WILDERNESS ENCOUNTER

My first realization, after an immediate stab of fear, was that the Indians wore no paint. There were stories enough in England about Indians painting for war.

"Put your weapons out of sight," I said, "below the gun-whales. I think they are peaceful."

The canoes slowed their pace, gliding down to us, and then a hand lifted, palm outward, and I recognized Potaka.

"It is my friend," I explained.

Rufisco snorted. "No Indian is your friend," he said. "Keep your gun handy."

"This is L'Amour plotting at breakneck speed,
writing lean and hard fiction,
all muscle and bone."
—Los Angeles Times

Sackett's Land

Louis L'Amour

SACKETT'S LAND
A Bantam Book

PRINTING HISTORY

Saturday Review Press edition published May 1974
2nd printing ...... November 1974
Literary Guild edition published October 1974
Bantam edition | May 1975

2nd printing	*........... May 1975*	*6th printing*	*........... June 1977*
3rd printing	*........... June 1975*	*7th printing*	*.. September 1977*
4th printing	*....... August 1975*	*8th prinitng*	*........... April 1978*
5th printing	*.. November 1976*	*9th printing*	*...... January 1979*

ISBN 0-553-12828-0

Published simultaneously in the United States and Canada

Bantam Books are published by Bantam Books, Inc. Its trademark, consisting of the words "Bantam Books" and the por-
trayal of a bantam, is Registered in U.S. Patent and Trademark
Office and in other countries. Marca Registrada. Bantam
Books, Inc., 666 Fifth Avenue, New York, New York 10019.

PRINTED IN THE UNITED STATES OF AMERICA

Preface

We are all of us, it has been said, the children of immigrants and foreigners—even the American Indian, although he arrived here a little earlier. What a man is and what he becomes is in part due to his heritage, and the men and women who came west did not emerge suddenly from limbo. Behind them were ancestors, families, and former lives. Yet even as the domestic cattle of Europe evolved into the wild longhorns of Texas, so the American pioneer had the characteristics of a distinctive type.

Physically and psychologically, the pioneers' need for change had begun in the old countries with their decision to migrate. In most cases their decisions were personal, ordered by no one else. Even when migration was ordered or forced, the people who survived were characterized by physical strength, the capacity to endure, and not uncommonly, a rebellious nature.

History is not made only by kings and parliaments, presidents, wars, and generals. It is the story of people, of their love, honor, faith, hope and suffering; of birth and death, of hunger, thirst and cold, of loneliness and sorrow. In writing my stories I have found myself looking back again and again to origins, to find and clearly see the ancestors of the pioneers.

Some time ago, I decided to tell the story of the American frontier through the eyes of three families —fictional families, but with true and factual experiences. The names I chose were Sackett, Chantry, and Talon. There is a real Sackett family my research revealed, which derives from the Isle of Ely, in Cambridgeshire, England. For historical accuracy I decided to bring my fictional Sacketts from the same area.

Cambridgeshire is fen-county—low, boggy land partially covered with water, and the fen-men were men of independent mind, as are my fictional Sacketts. They were also hunters and fishermen, which was important, though few of those who first landed in America had any idea of how to survive. In a land teeming with game, with edible wild plants, many were starving in the midst of plenty, and had to learn hunting and fishing from the Indians.

Story by story, generation by generation, these families are moving westward. When the journeys are ended and the forty-odd books are completed, the reader should have a fairly true sense of what happened on the American frontier.

The story that follows is of the first Sackett to come to America.

Chapter 1

It was my devil's own temper that brought me to grief, my temper and a skill with weapons born of my father's teaching.

Yet without that skill I might have emptied my life's blood upon the cobblestones of Stamford, emptied my body of blood . . . and for what?"

Until that moment in Stamford it would have been said that no steadier lad lived in all the fen-lands than Barnabas Sackett, nor one who brought better from his fields than I, or did better at the eeling in the fens that were my home.

Then a wayward glance from a lass, a moment of red, bursting fury from a stranger, a blow given and a blow returned, and all that might have been my life vanished like a fog upon the fens beneath a summer sun.

In that year of 1599 a man of my station did not strike a man of noble birth and expect to live—or if he lived, to keep the hand that struck the blow.

Trouble came quickly upon me, suddenly, and without warning.

It began that day near Reach when I slipped and fell upon the Devil's Dyke.

The Dyke is a great rampart of earth some six miles long and built in the long ago by a people who might have been my ancestors. These were the Iceni,

1

I have been told, who lived in my country long before the Romans came to Britain.

When I slipped I caught myself upon my outstretched palms to keep the mud from my clothing, and I found myself staring at the muddy edge of what appeared to be a gold coin.

Now coins of any kind were uncommon amongst us, for we did much in the way of barter and exchange. Merchants saw coins, but not many came our way. Yet here it was, a gold coin.

Shifting my position a bit I closed my fingers over first one coin and, then, yet another.

I stood up slowly, and making as if to brush the mud from my hands, I knocked and wiped the mud from the coins. In a pool of muddy water at my feet, I washed them clean.

They were old . . . very, very old.

No English coins these, nor was the wording English, nor the faces of the men upon them. The first coin was heavy, of quite some value judging by the weight. The second was smaller, thinner, and of a different kind.

Slipping them casually into my pocket, I stood there looking about.

The hour was before dawn of what bid to be a gray day. Clouds were thick above, and during the night there had been heavy rain. It was a lonely place, where I stood, a place about half the distance from Reach to Wood Ditton. We had worked in the quarries at Reach, some of us, and slept the night on a tavern floor to be near the fire.

Long before day I awakened, lying there thinking of the distance I had yet to go, with the work now ended. So, quietly I had risen, put my cloak about my shoulders, and took my way to the Dyke, the easiest route in any weather.

It was a time when few men got more than a mile or two from their door, unless following the sea or the fishing, but I was a restless one, moving about and working wherever an extra hand might be needed, for it was in my mind to save money, buy a bit more land and so better my position.

Now I had come upon gold, more than I was likely to earn with my hands in a year, although it was little enough I knew of gold. Had my father stood by me he could have told me what each coin was worth.

I made a thing of brushing my knees, which gave me time to look more carefully about.

I was alone. There were willows yonder, farther away oaks and a hedge, but nowhere in the vague light of beginning day did I see movement or sign of men. Carefully I studied the ground where I had fallen. For where there had been two coins there might be three . . . or four.

Something had scarred the slope here, and rain had found it, as rain will, gouging a small ditch to escape over the Dyke's edge. Where the trickle of water was, I could see what appeared to be the rotting edge of a leather purse, or sack. A bit of a search with my fingers in the mud and I held three more pieces of gold, and a moment later, another.

That was the lot. I kicked mud over the spot, turned about a couple of times, then walked slowly on, plodding as if tired, stopping a time or two to look about.

At a pool of rain water I paused to wash the mud from my hands. Six gold coins! It was a fortune.

Two of the coins were Roman. Likely enough some

brawny legionnaire had come this way from the fighting, and when about to be overtaken had buried
them. It was likely he must have been killed then,
for he had never recovered his coins.

Such a strong leather purse, if well buried, would
need years to rot away, and it might have been some
later traveler. Whoever it was, his ancient loss was
my present gain.

Yet if I appeared with six gold coins, what would
happen?

By some manner of means they would certainly be
taken from me. A poor man, even a yeoman such
as I, had small chance of maintaining his rights. There
were many tricky laws, and the rascals would surely
find one that would deprive me of my findings.

I was a freeman living on a small freeholding at the
edge of the fens, a bit of land given my father for
his deeds in battle. Actually, a great piece of the
fens was mine, but it was of small use except for the
eeling and occasional mowing.

There was a small piece of land adjoining mine, of
good, rich drained land that I coveted. Now I could
have it for mine, and more, too, if it were up for
the selling.

But if I came forward with gold it would set to
wagging half the tongues in the shire, so I had best
be thinking of a better way.

It was then I remembered the man from Stamford.
An oldish man, and bookish. His name had been
mentioned to me in the streets of Chatteris. A curious
man, he would go miles to look upon some old wall
or a ruined monastery.

His name was Hasling, and sometimes he had
bought some ancient thing found by a workman or

farmer. It was said he wrote papers about such things and talked of them with men from Cambridge.

He had the look of a kindly man with nothing of the sharper about him, and I'd been told he paid a guinea for a bronze axe dug up in a field. So it was that I went to Stamford.

It was no great house I came to but a fine, comfortable cottage, early in the day. A cottage with fine old trees about and a deal of lawn behind. There were flowers planted and birds who made themselves at home.

When I put knuckles to the door a woman in a white cap opened it, a pleasant-faced woman with a look of the Irish about her, but no friendly smile for me, in my rough dress.

When I spoke of business with Coveney Hasling she looked doubtful, but when I said it was an old thing I had to speak of, the door was wide at once, and the next thing I knew I was seated with a cup of tea in my hand, although I'd have preferred it to be ale.

The room had papers and books all about, a skull with a cleft in it giving me the round eye from black and empty sockets. Close by a bronze axe . . . the very one.

It was in my mind to question whether the cleft skull and the bronze axe had ever met before when he came in, bowing a short bow and peering at me with tilted head. "Yes, yes, lad, you wished to speak to me?"

"Aye. I have heard you spoken of as one with an interest in old things."

"You have found something!" He was excited as a child. "What is it? Let me see!"

"I'd have to ask your silence. I'd not be losing the profit of it."

"Profit? Profit, do you say? It is history you must think of, lad, history!"

"History you may think of, who live in a fine house. Profit is my concern, who does not."

"You are a freeman?"

"With a small holding."

"I see. Come, come! Sit you down! You get about some, I take it. Do you know the Roman roads?"

"I do, and the dykes and walls as well. Some earthworks, too, and I might even know a floor of Roman tile."

"Lad, lad! You could be of service to me and your country as well! These things you speak of . . . they must not be lost or destroyed. They are a part of our heritage!"

"No doubt, but it is my own heritage I be thinking of now. I have your silence then?"

"You do."

From my pocket I took the first coin, and he took it reverently to hand, going off to the window for light. He exclaimed with pleasure, "You would sell this?"

"I would."

"Is there more? Or is this all?"

When I hesitated, his eyes twinkled. "You asked for silence. I have given my word."

"There are six coins in all, but they are not alike."

"I should be surprised if they were. Roman soldiers were from many lands, and they marched and fought in many more. They gambled with each other with coins of many kinds."

"I brought only one other coin."

He took the second, examined it at the window light, then returned to the table.

The room was furnished in the fashion of the time, and the furniture was old. When entering I had seen

6

a great box chair in the entrance way, a cumbersome thing that would take two strong men to carry. At the table, however, were three chairs of a more recent style with leather seats and backs.

Obviously he slept in another room, but there was a great chest here of the kind men had slept upon in my father's boyhood. Of late they had begun putting drawers in the chest, and most were used for storage as well as sleeping. The tapestries on the wall were the work of Sheldon of Warwick, excellently done. In other homes I had visited they were often painted on cloth or leather.

"What of the other coins?"

"Let us speak first of these."

Hasling chuckled. "Lad, I like you. You have told no one of these coins?"

"No."

"It is better so. Gold is not that common amongst us, even with the treasure from the Spanish ships that Master Drake has been bringing us. I could afford to buy no more than one of these coins, although I have a friend, also an antiquarian, who collects coins."

He looked at me from under heavy brows. "Would you have some more tea, lad?"

When I nodded he called for the woman, and she came bearing the pot. It was a guilty feeling I had, drinking tea like it was water. For what a pound of tea cost a man might rent five acres for a year, and the bit of land I had from my father, the land outside the fens, was scarcely five acres with a cottage and a stable.

Of course, there were some hidden acres in the fen, but of them I told nobody, and few indeed knew of them. The fen was a vast marsh land, heavily saturated with water. Here and there were outcroppings of limestone, and also some islands used by smugglers occasionally, and known only to we of the fens.

"Do you know aught of the Romans?" he asked me.

"Aye. My father was a soldier and he gathered tales of the Romans, how they marched and built their camps and drank vinegar when athirst."

"They conquered the world," Hasling said.

"Only a piece of it," I objected, remembering what my father had taught me. "They knew of Cathay, but never marched against it."

Hasling chuckled, obviously pleased. "You are right, lad, and not many know of that, even at Cambridge. You are a uncommon fen-man."

"There are uncommon men everywhere, so many that the common man has become uncommon."

He glanced at me, then turned back to the coins. "Your father was a soldier? And your name is . . . ?"

"Barnabas Sackett. There is another family of the name in Ely, but we are not related. My father was Ivo Sackett.

"Ivo Sackett! Of course! Your father made a name for himself. He is remembered."

"I know he went to the wars."

"Aye, and how he went to them! He was a rare man, your father." He glanced at me again. "The other coins? You can bring them to me?"

"I can. When I have the silver for these."

He left the room and returning, paid me a goodly sum. "Take this," he said, "and rest assured I am your friend. Bring me the other coins and I will have a purchaser for them. Antiquities may have only a small market in England, lad, but there's a few of us fancy the old things."

He held up the coins. "These are a part of our history in the world, and from such as these we can piece together a forgotten story. Men have lived and died in England these thousands of years and each of them may have left something more than his dust. Fitted together, these things may compose forgotten chapters of our history."

History is best made by men with hands. Brains are well enough, but count for nothing without the hands to build, to bring to fulfilment. Willing as I was to listen to ancient history, at this moment my interest centered upon my own, a history lived until this moment in more modest circumstances than I would wish.

With the money I now had, I could purchase from William those adjoining acres, and hold enough land to live as a yeoman should. Yet even as I thought of this, another thought forced itself into my head, bringing discontent: Was this all? Was there no more for me?

My father had been a soldier, wandering wide upon the world; yet what had he said to me? "Own a few acres, lad, and keep it unencumbered and you'll not want for some'at to eat. You can always grow a few cabbages."

Aye, if cabbages would suffice. To hold the acres, yes, but to move out from them . . . that was what I felt I must do.

William was a steady man, and if I chose to go wide upon the world for a small bit he would work my acres and hold them for me and perhaps a sum as well.

These were my thoughts as I said good-bye to the Haslings.

Scarcely had I left the Hasling cottage when trouble fell upon me. Walking across the town toward the highroad, and passing by the tavern, I looked up and into the eyes of a girl.

She sat in a carriage before the tavern and when I looked, she seemed to smile.

Now there was an exuberance upon me. Gaiety and good will were in my blood. My pockets jingled with more coin than I'd had in many a year past, and more to come.

She was no child, this one. A girl, but a woman also, and of rare beauty. So when she smiled, I smiled in return, and doffed my hat as bravely as though it were plumed.

She was of the gentry, it went without saying. A carriage was a rare thing, and few possessed them or had the use of one. She was gentry, and the less one noticed or was noticed by them the better. I was passing when her low voice said, "I am thirsty."

What was I to do? The well was there, its water cold and fresh. Filling a brimming dipper, I took it to her.

I was holding the dipper out to her when it was struck from my hand, a vicious, stinging blow.

Turning sharply, I faced a young noble wearing a plumed hat such as I did not have, his face flushed with anger.

"Carrion! Why, you vulgar . . . !" He struck at my face with a gloved hand, but instinctively, knowing something of fisticuffs, I dodged. Missing the blow he fell into the mud.

I laughed . . . and she laughed as well.

For an instant he glared at me from the mud, and then with a burst of fury he came off the ground. In the next instant he had drawn his sword.

She screamed. "Rupert! *No!*" And he lunged at me.

That he was beyond reason was obvious. Also that he intended to kill me.

It was my father's training that saved me. Although I wore no sword I carried a blackthorn stick, and automatically I parried and thrust, the end of my stick taking him fairly in the wind.

He staggered and went down.

A rough hand grasped my arm. "You daft fool! That's Rupert Genester, nephew to the Earl!"

Chapter 2

There was an opening in the gathering crowd. I took it. There was a space between the houses, I went through it. There was an open lane under the trees. I went down it.

Many were my faults, but lack of decision was not one of them. Why Genester, if such was his name, had struck me I did not know, unless he feared contamination of his lady by one of such modest birth as myself.

He had struck me, and worst of all, I struck him back, knocked him down, and to compound my errors, I laughed at him, as his lady had laughed. In his place I might have been furious, too.

Decision had been imperative. My actions had been purely reflex, instinctive responses. To strike was to parry, to parry was to thrust . . . these impulses lay in my muscles and that part of my brain that directed them. When he came up from the ground he had intended to kill me.

As I ran, someone came abreast of me. "This way!" he gasped. "Through the trees!"

Great old trees bordered the lane. He dodged between them and led the way across an open field. We walked a while to catch our wind.

"I have a horse," he said.

Beside a tumbled ruin, within a shady place, his horse grazed. I did not ask why he had left his horse hidden in such a place. But for the first time I did get a good look at the man who was helping me escape.

He was a slender, wiry man, not yet so tall as me, of sallow complexion, eyes black and deep-sunk. He looked to be a shrewd and careful man. He carried a sword, which at the moment I envied, and a Florentine dagger. Its mate was in my cottage near Isleham, on the fens.

"One horse?" I asked.

"We will take turns, running and riding. We can travel quite fast."

He insisted that I mount, and I did. We emerged from the hidden place and into another lane, he trotting alongside and clinging to the stirrup-leather. When we had gone a half-mile we changed places, me running alongside.

During one such change he said to me, "I regret I can offer no place where we would be safe. This land is strange to me."

"Worry not over that," I told him. "I have such a place, where none will follow."

My thoughts had been busy. Who in Stamford might know me? None but Hasling and his housekeeper, and not even they knew where lay my home. Not many people traveled so there was a goodly chance none of those who had witnessed my deed had seen me before, or my village. Yet if such there was, once I reached the fens I was lost to them.

For the fens were a vast area of low-lying ground, of shallow lakes and winding waterways, impassable swamps with here and there limestone outcroppings that created small islands, often with clumps of birch or ancient oaks.

From a distance the fens were deceptively flat and uninteresting, but once down in the winding waterways, they proved anything but that. For there were clumps of willow and alder, or tall reeds that permitted boats to move about almost unseen. The scattered islands in the vastness of the fens were mostly secret, a knowledge reserved for fen-men alone, places of refuge in time of trouble. Most of the waterways were hidden by reeds up to ten feet tall.

Bog myrtle, bladderwort, marsh fern, saw sedge and dozens of varieties of plants and shrubs grew there, and we of the fens knew them all. It was there the Iceni had gone to escape the attacks of northern sea-rovers who invaded the land by sailing up the Ouse or the Cam.

Our fens were sparsely inhabited by a clannish lot who cared not for outsiders coming to our watery world.

We left Lincolnshire behind, my companion and I, traveling devious ways. I led the way to Thorney, a lovely village with a great old abbey and many sheltered places where a man might keep from sight. We had no desire to leave behind us those who might speak of our passing.

In a wooded copse, a hollow among the hills, we built a small fire and tethered our horse.

"I am Barnabas Sackett," I said. "I have a place on the edge of the fens. We will go there."

"I am Jublain. My family, it is said, came from Mayenne, but that was long ago. I am from nowhere in particular."

"A man is what he is."

"A profound saying. You have the manner and the shoulders of a fighting man. You are a soldier?"

"I am a farmer. I have a small holding."

"You moved swiftly. It was beautiful, Barnabas . . . beautiful!"

"He would have killed me."

"He would that. It was in his eye when he came up from the mud. He did not like being made ridiculous, and not knowing you, I thought you were a dead man."

From his saddlebags he took a chunk of bread and broke it in two, handing the half to me. It was old bread and hard, but it tasted well, very well.

"I have no wine." He glanced at me. "I have eaten little these past few weeks. These are bitter times for a masterless man."

"Wait. We will have enough to eat."

"They will search for you. You know that?"

"Do you know aught of the fens? They'll not find me, not in a hundred years. Mile upon mile of deep marsh, willows, alders, and channels. Places where you can walk for several hundred yards, then drop through the grass into a hole large enough to take a cathedral. We will go there."

I paused, considering. "Yet I do not believe any in Stamford knew me. I was there on business."

"And he whom you saw on business? He will not speak?"

"I think not. He seemed a good man, but one who would keep silent. And there is reason for his silence, a good reason."

He looked at me but I did not explain. One does not tell a stranger with a dagger and a sword that one has gold.

"Still, a man of your size, with your skill at arms. . . ."

"Nobody knows my skill. Not even my friends. My father taught me at home when none were about. There are few who know me. Some know I own land; most only that I have worked in the quarries."

"Your father was a soldier?"

"Yes."

"A neat parry," Jublain muttered. "I'd have taken you for a swordsman."

"I am a farmer," I insisted, "planning to buy a cow and a few acres more."

"A *cow?*" Jublain was scornful. "In your position I'd choose a blade. You'll have more need of it, for all your swamps."

"I have a sword, and no good it does me, hanging upon the wall. In truth, three of them I have, a halberd as well, a brace of pistols and a fowling piece."

"What kind of a farmer are you who goes armed like a pirate?"

"My father took the weapons in battle. One sword was given him by a great Earl."

"A likely tale!"

"An Earl," I replied with dignity, "who would have died had not my father stood over him on the field and slain nine enemies who would have killed him as he lay helpless. The Earl gave him a sword,

15

a purse of gold with which he bought our land, and promises which I have forgotten."

"It is as well. Such men are free with promises and freer at forgetting them."

"I have the sword."

"You'd best wear it, then."

"A farmer with a sword? Folk would think me daft."

"Better daft than dead. You've made an enemy, my friend, who will neither forgive nor forget. My advice is carry the sword, charge the pistols, and sleep not too well."

We talked long, then slept. But before the light of dawn, we were upon our way. Then I led him into the fens, and a long way it was, by such routes as only then fen-men knew.

I had no fear of pursuit. A step or two to right or left might put a man over his head in an ugly tangle of roots, floating plants and decaying, matted reeds. But there were safe and certain ways to be followed by the knowing, and the grass had a way of springing back up when one passed, leaving no trail to be followed by a stranger.

Three days we traveled before reaching my cottage, and a neat place it was, my father being a man of judgment in such matters. The cottage was of four rooms, large for its time, with a stable for animals separate from the house. The cottage was of limestone quarried on the spot, with a roof of deep thatch, tight and well made.

"A tidy place," Jublain said, "a right tidy place."

When I had lighted a candle he looked at the swords on the wall. First was the gift from the Earl, a straight, double-edged weapon with a good point. The second a Turkish scimitar, engraved and beautiful, and the third a falchion, broad-bladed, incredibly sharp.

"You did not lie," Jublain admitted reluctantly. "These are blades!"

"My father took the scimitar from a Turk at Lepanto. He was also at the victory over the French at Saint-Quentin, and at the Battle of Zutphen. There were others . . . many others."

"That's a spread of years," Jublain acknowledged.

"He went to the wars at seventeen, and was a soldier until three years before he died. I have heard he was a noted fighting man."

There was food enough in the house, meal, cheese, dried fish and the like. I put them together and went to the cool place near the well where I kept my ale.

Then we sat down to eat.

If he could fight like he ate, this Jublain was a noted warrior himself; but well as he ate, he drank even better. With a cup of ale in him he talked well of wars and weals and bloody times gone by. The stories were like my father's tales, but with my father each tale had a point for my instruction; he seemed to know his time was short and he wished to pass on what he could. He wished me not to go unarmed into the world, and warned me to prepare for wily men and wilier women, and to face danger with some knowledge and some art.

"All this I have learned," he told me one night, beside our fire, "and much more, but of what further use if I cannot pass it onto you. Learn from me and avoid the scars your soul and mind will take, let alone your body. Profit by what I say, Barnabas, and go on to learn new things, and when you have a son, teach him."

"I may not have a son."

"Have a son, by all means, but choose the lady well. Breeding counts for much in dogs, horses, and men. Breed for strength, health, and stamina, but for wisdom, too. Your mother was a better person than I, a clear-eyed one who saw to the truth of things, and I see much of you in her.

"You will see many women, and often you will think yourself in love, but temper passion with wisdom, my son, for sometimes the glands speak louder than the brain. Each man owes a debt to his family, his country and his species to leave sons and daughters who will lead, inspire and create."

He was a talker, my father, when we were alone, but sparing of words with others around. When he spoke of wars it was of what had been done, what might have been done, and what he believed should have been done.

"The art of war can be learned," he told me. "But after the principles are learned the rest is ingenuity, the gift that goes beyond learning, or the instinct born of understanding.

"There are good ways and bad ways of attacking fortified positions, of crossing streams under attack, or withdrawing when the situation is no longer favorable.

"Learn the accepted modes of attack and defense, then use the variations that are your own. Masters of battle know what has already been done, then go beyond it with skill and discretion. Alexander, Hannibal, Belisarius . . . study them. They were masters.

Of these things I spoke to Jublain, and he stared at me. "Your father was only a soldier? He should have been a captain himself."

"Captains' commands go to men of birth. My father

was a strong man with a sword . . . perhaps in another time, another place. . . ."

"Aye," Jublain muttered. He took a swallow of ale. "I think sometimes of the lands oversea. If rough soldiers such as Pizarro could do it, why not I? He had no particular birth, no position. He had only courage, will, and a sword."

"In a new land," I agreed, "all things are possible. I have given much thought to this. Perhaps in a new land only achievement would give rank, and not birth. To be born of an eminent family is nothing if you are nothing yourself."

"In a new land a man might become a king. He might take hold of land as did the Normans when they came to England, and the Saxons before them."

"I do not want to be a king," I said, "I want only freedom to grow and do and be as much as time will allow."

For two days we ate well and lived quietly. Jublain was content to rest, for there were cold, hungry days behind him, and as for me, there was much to do about the place. For months past I had worked in the quarries, with but few nights at home.

Suddenly my mind seemed to stop still.

There had been a man at Reach when I worked there . . . I had glimpsed his face in the crowd at Stamford.

Now I was uneasy. The man might not remember me, might not tell, might not even know where I came from. Still . . .

When Jublain was out of the cottage I took the other coins from their hiding place and hid them in a secret pocket in the seams of my clothing. Mayhap we might abandon this place, and I wished to be ready.

Then, on the fourth day, a drum of hoofs awakened me before the light. Stepping from my bed I took down the Earl's sword, then placed it upon the table and stepped outside.

The air was cool and damp. Fog lay upon the fens, beading my grass with dew and making the grass itself greener where it could be seen at all.

The drum of hoofs slowed and a rider came down to the fence and stopped at the gate. When he opened the gate and led his horse through, he turned. It was Coveney Hasling.

He wasted no time. "You are in trouble, lad, serious trouble. You were known to someone and by tomorrow he and other men will have made inquiries at Reach. Then they will come here."

"It was good of you to come."

"You will need money." He took a handful of coins from his pocket. "Take this and pay me when you sell what you have, but be gone from here. Into the fens with you."

"I shall do that, but you have ridden far. Come . . . we will eat first. I have found it is better to eat when one can, for one never knows when he will eat again."

He tied his horse and entered the cottage with me. Jublain was up, holding a naked sword.

"Jublain is a soldier," I explained. "Jublain, my friend from Stamford. He carries a warning."

Hasling's eyes swept the cottage, rested upon the sword. "That will be it, then? The blade given your father by the Earl?"

"It is," I said.

"I know the story," Hasling said, to my surprise. "I was reminded of it when your name was mentioned. I know a friend of yours."

"Of mine?"

"The man who buys antiquities. He knew your father."

"Barnabas has an enemy, too," Jublain said, irritably. "What of him?"

"Rupert Genester? An evil man, but one with power in many places. You could have no worse an enemy. He is an ambitious man, an heir, a man filled with pride and hatred. He was laughed at and that he cannot abide."

We drank our ale, then Hasling mounted and was gone, returning by a different route that I suggested.

Standing at the gate, I listened to the beat of hoofs as his horse carried him away. Walking back to the cottage I belted on a sword and dagger. I charged the pistols afresh while Jublain watched me, his eyes bright with irony.

"You learn quickly." He emptied his cup.

We among the fens were an independent lot. We were a people who *did*, with contempt for all who did nothing.

For centuries smugglers had used the fens, bringing their craft up the secret waterways. We paid them no mind, but knew them and their ways. Few of us entered the army, fewer were impressed into the fleet. We went our ways, content with them.

From a chest I took a casque that had belonged to my father, and the weapons from the walls. I took bacon, hams, dried fruit, cheese, and meal. We loaded them into my punt.

Returning to close the door of the cottage, I was turning from it when they rushed upon me, a half-dozen armed men. They came at me, and my sword was out.

"Kill him! I want him *dead!* Do you hear?"

I heard the shout as they closed, but when battle was joined I was not one to dally about, so I had at them, sidestepping to place one between myself and the others, parrying his thrust and thrusting my own sword home with one movement.

Quickly withdrawing my blade as the man fell, I had a moment when they hesitated. Shocked to see one of their own die, for they had come to murder a farmer, not to die themselves, they paused, appalled. It was the moment I needed, and with a shout, I went at them.

I feinted, thrust . . . the sword went deep. Then they were all about me and my sword was everywhere, parrying, thrusting, knowing I could not continue long, when suddenly there was a shout from behind.

"Have at them, men!" It was Jublain. "Let not one escape!"

They broke and fled. Murder is one thing, a fight another. They had the stomach for one, only their heels for the other. They did not wait to see if there were more than two, but fled, unheeding their master's angry shouts.

As they fled we ran toward our punt. Three men were down and a fourth had staggered as they fled. I heard a voice call out:

"I know you now! I know you forever, and you shall not escape!"

It was Rupert Genester.

Chapter 3

The country of the fens was not so large as most of us believed it to be, but to us it seemed endless, a vast, low-lying, and marshy land where remnants grew of the once great forest that had covered England.

The Romans, who understood the reclaiming of marshy land, had begun the drainage of the fens, but once they departed the Saxons let the canals fill and the fens return to fens.

It was said that even now Queen Bess was talking to a Dutch engineer, a man with much experience at draining land below sea level. This we did not oppose, for reclaiming land might make some of us rich.

Myself, for instance. I owned but a few acres of tillable land, but owned by grant more than two square miles of fen. Once drained, such rich land would make me wealthy.

Yet I was now a fugitive. Had my case come to trial it might possibly have turned out well for me. Occasionally a commoner won such a case, but the occasions were too rare to make me confident. I had the thought that it would never come to court, for the hand of Rupert Genester could reach even into prison to kill me, easily.

For some time I rowed until Jublain asked impatiently, "Are you lost, man? You are rowing in circles."

"Almost a circle," I agreed cheerfully, "but not lost."

Fog lay thick down the tips of the blades of grass. No movement was in the water, no sound but the chunk of my oars in the locks, and that to be heard no more than a few feet away.

Where we now went was a place I had played in as a child, visiting but rarely since. It was an islet of perhaps three acres, cut by several narrow, winding waterways. It was an outcropping of limestone with a few birch trees and some ancient, massive oaks, thickly-branched. Reaching the place I sought—where an old snag of a dead tree projected upward from the bog—I turned past it, parted the reeds and took the boat into a hidden waterway which I followed for almost a hundred feet. There, against a limestone shelf, I moored the punt to an iron ring.

Taking weapons and food we walked the narrow path between limestone boulders and trees to a small shelf backed up against a fifteen-foot cliff of the same material. There stood a small hut, also of limestone, thatched and secure.

"This is mine," I told him.

"You do yourself well," he admitted grudgingly.

"We may have to drive out bats or water rats," I said, but we did not. It was tight and snug as always; a deep fireplace, thick walls, a table, two chairs, two chests on which to sleep and a bench along the wall. There was also a cupboard.

Gathering fuel together I kindled a small fire to take off the chill. "It is an ancient place," I said, "the men of the fens hid here from the Romans."

"And well they could do it," Jublain admitted. "A man would have the devil's own time finding a way to come in."

For the time being we were safe. This had been

a snug haven even from the Danes. When they had finally captured the Isle of Ely after their first defeat they had never found this place. The house, old as it was, had been rebuilt, patched and repaired time and again.

Yet I had no idea of hiding forever in the fens, especially with more money in pocket than I'd ever had before. The events of the past few days had caused me to reexamine my life and choose a course I could steer with safety.

Pulling an oar through the dark channels had given me time to think, and my thoughts had taken a sudden turn. Perhaps the use of the sword had inspired it; more likely the jingle of coins!

"We will lie quiet and fish for a few days," I told Jublain. "Then off for London."

"London? Are you daft, man? That is where Genester will be, and where he is strongest."

"It is a vast city," I said complacently. "Folk say more than one hundred thousand people live there. How could I be found among so many?"

"You are a child," Jublain said angrily. "It is too small a place in which to hide from hate."

"I've a few coins," I said, "and I'm of no mind to rot in the fens. I do not wish to spend my life fishing or hunting with the bow."

"You are an archer, too?"

"So is every man in the fens. We can live by the bow."

"Let us off to the wars, then. We might do uncommon well."

"And lose an arm or an eye? No, I'll go a-venturing, but with goods, not my life."

"You'd become a merchant? A *trader?*"

"Why not? Buy a packet of goods and ship as a

merchant venturer for the New World. There's a man named Gosnold, Bartholomew Gosnold, a gentleman from Suffolk. He has it in mind to start a colony there. There's wealth in trading with the Indians, he says."

"Bah!" Jublain was impatient. "Idle talk! Who knows what is there? The Spanish have done well, but north of their lands there is nothing but cold forests and hostile savages."

"And furs," I said.

"You live well here," he said. "You'd be a fool to give it up."

"There's geese," I admitted, "and ducks and fish and wild plants and eels. Or if a man was so inclined he could smuggle."

"But not you?" he asked cynically.

"I've a regard for law, although I do not always agree with it. Without law, man becomes a beast."

Jublain stared, then shrugged. "You are an odd one. All right, if it is London you wish for, to London we will go, but remember what I said. It is a small town when you are hated."

Outside, we tried our swords. Jublain was good, skilled in ways in which I was not. Yet soon I realized I was his master, and deliberately held back because I valued his friendship. He was a difficult man, cross-grained, cynical, a scoffer. He seemed to believe in nothing but fighting, wandering, drinking, and wenching. So I took my practice with him, tried to learn, and refused to show the limits of my skill.

To me, one hundred thousand people was a multitude. Between London and us, England was heavily forested with stretches of wild moorland and the marshy wastes of the fens. Roads were mere cart tracks or trails, wandering by the easiest routes through the forests and across the land. All were infested with thieves and highwaymen.

These things my father had told me. There were scattered farms, a few great estates. A few old Roman roads were still in use. New roads were often knee-deep in mud.

Waterways would offer the easiest route across country, but any travel was a hardship. Most who traveled understood why the word "travel" had once been "travail."

"We will go by sea," I said.

"A ship will be hard to come by in these fens," Jublain said wryly.

"We're not over-far from Boston, from which sail many ships, but I've a thought we need not even go so far. We'll put the word out, my friend, and catch a ship off the River Nene."

Inside, the fire crackled in the fireplace and the warm glow had driven the damp chill from the little house. There was wood enough close by, I'd seen to that. We carried in several armsful and dropped them near the hearth.

"If you've a notion of hunting treasure," I said, "you can always look for the Royal Crown jewels lost by King John, crossing the Wash. So far as anyone knows they still lie in the mud there, for no man has ever found them. King John died only a short time after. . . ."

"I've heard men speak of those jewels. What a pretty find they would be!"

"Don't trouble yourself. By now they're deep sunk in mud or washed out to sea. Someday they'll be found, but a long time from now, I'm thinking, and by accident."

I cut thick slices from a ham and tossed them into

a pan for frying. It was warm and snug within and the fog was still thick without—it might hang on for days.

"Do you know London?" I asked him.

"A bit. There are some inns, but better are the places kept by soldiers' wives; they are cleaner, I am thinking. But the White Hart in Southwark is a likely place, or the Tabard, near London Bridge."

"Good! Within three days then."

Long it had been in my thoughts to see London, for there was much I had to learn, and inquiries to make of the New World. Perhaps I could talk to Gosnold himself.

Some new clothing first. What I wore was not good enough for London . . . for the places I wished to go . . . for Gosnold.

Yet even as I thought, I looked quickly around. Would I ever come back to this? Was I leaving it only for now? Or forever?

Was I deliberately venturing into London because of Genester's threat?

No! I examined myself carefully and found no challenge there. Genester was not important to me. What was important was that I improve myself and my condition.

My father had taught me much of arms and fighting. Laboriously and through long hours he had taught me to read and write. He had schooled me in manners. He had given me the knowledge and skills that could make me an officer and a gentleman. . . . Was I to waste them here? This much *he* had done. It was up to me to take the next step.

"Give a thought to your future, Jublain," I said. "You need not always be only a soldier nor I a man of the fens. I intend one day to have a name and an estate."

He smiled thinly, his eyes taunting. "You have large ideas. I have heard them before . . . many times."

"I will do it, Jublain."

He glanced at me thoughtfully. "You might, at that. After all, some of the great families of the world were founded with nothing but a sword and a strong right arm."

"I shall found a family," I said, "but not with a sword."

Jublain shrugged. "You might do it, but keep the sword at hand. You'll need it."

Chapter 4

The tavern we chose in Southwark was a great, rambling old structure with a large wagon yard, a double row of balconies hanging over the yard, and on the ground floor, a room where drinks were served —a warm and friendly place. In an adjoining room, meals were served.

Business was brisk. Horsemen came and went at all hours. Wagons, carts, and, more rarely, carriages came into the yard.

Despite his hesitation about claiming a knowledge of London, Jublain guided me to a tailor where I outfitted myself with a rich but modest wardrobe, equipping Jublain with a few items of which he was in need.

"You'll have no money at this rate," Jublain warned. "If you're to go a-venturing you'll be needing it all to buy goods."

He was right, of course, but there'd been a thought stirring around in my skull. That evening I wrote a message to Hasling.

If you wish to talk of Romans or antiquities, I shall be some nights at the Tabard, near London Bridge.

This message I forwarded, unsigned. None knew of my interest in antiquities but Hasling, nor that I was in London. I saw no easy way in which the message could be traced back to me, yet I was worried. Despite his foppish dress, Genester had the look of a shrewd one.

Jublain and I no longer looked like country bumpkins. Attired like gentlemen we could go where we wished, but the public room at the inn was a hotbed of gossip and information, so we loitered there, that first day, listening to talk of roads, people, and politics, of the theater, bear-baitings, brawls, and robberies.

"Gosnold?" It was the reply to a casual comment of mine. "Oh, aye! He'll be going yon. Newport, also. He has a letter from the Queen and can take prizes. If you be the sort with a taste for action, he's your man.

"There's others stirring about you'd best beware of. Cap'n Nick Bardle . . . no better than a pirate. He's outfitting this minute and will be off to the coast of America. The man's nae to be trusted. Take the coppers from a dead man's eyes, he would, and might even hasten the dying.

"He's got a bad lot sailing with him and if he's a man short he'll just knock some poor duffer on the head and before he comes to his senses he's at sea."

"If it's venturing you want," Jublain said, "it must be Gosnold or Newport, or Weymouth when he gets in. All have sailed the coast of America, all are solid men."

Yet I was thinking of something else. Hasling's quickness to buy my coins excited my interest in antiquities. If he was interested—and his unnamed friend, too—others would be. Here was a market ready to be supplied by a man with a quick eye who could get around the country.

Casually, I mentioned buyers of old things. "Aye," a drover told me, "there be plenty. They've a society that meets to talk of such things. They'll chatter like magpies over an old coin, a chair or a casque."

Here might be a source of income unsuspected, for the gentry rarely knew the back roads as did we who labored with our hands. Nor did they suspect the number of dealers in junk who bought all manner of things from peasants, gypsies, and vagabonds. I had been to such places searching for tools, and had seen oddments lying about of no interest to anyone.

Of no interest to me either, then. Now I began to see that if a man had some knowledge, and a little money, then he might find, buy and sell to a substantial profit.

I remembered then that my father had once told of a man who devoted much of his life to wandering about compiling notes for a history of England. He had walked the cart roads and lanes, roamed along the seashore, and explored many ruins left unnoticed before his time. My father had traveled with him a time or two for a few days. His name, I recalled, was John Leland.

He died well before my time and before his history was written, but his notes had been copied.

Now if I could come upon such a copy . . .

Frequently I'd seen a man about the public room at the inn who eyed me from time to time with a quizzical cast to his eye. He had the look of a rogue, and I'd no doubt he was one, but he struck me as an amusing and interesting fellow. So when he next looked regretfully into the bottom of his glass, I suggested he have another.

He accepted quickly enough, and I said, "You have the look of a man who knows what's about."

"Here and there," he admitted.

"There was a man named John Leland who wrote some notes for a book about England. I'd like a copy of them."

"A copy of a book?" he started at me, then shook his head. "I know nought of such things." He looked up from his glass. "It comes upon me that I know a man who once said he'd copy anything for a price, and reasonable enough, too."

"You have a glass of ale," I said, "and you can have another, or a meal if you like. Who is this man?"

He glanced right and left, yet I believe it was the looks of Jublain, not too unlike his own kind, that won him in the end. "Do you know Saint Paul's Walk?"

"I do," said Jublain.

"There be scribes there, and there be one scribe who . . . well, what you need done, he will do. He knows much of books and such. If it is a copy of something, he'll find it for you."

"What is it to be? The meal or the ale?"

He grinned, his teeth yellow and broken. "I'd prefer the drink but I need the meat."

When I had ordered, I asked, "The name?"

"Ask for Peter Tallis. If it be an altered bill of lading, a warrant or a license, he will have it for you."

When we were outside Jublain looked at me, exasperated. "You are an odd one. Who would pay for the copy of some idle notes?"

"Watch me," I replied cheerfully. "I will pay."

Saint Paul's Walk was where London's heart could be heard beating. Actually, it was the nave of the great cathedral, but forgetting that Jesus had driven the moneylenders from the temple, the Dean had welcomed them back, and with them had come the scribes, the lawyers, sellers of badges and souvenirs, and, in fact, every sort of business. The playing of ball was forbidden, as was the riding or leading of horses.

It had become the greatest promenade in London, haunted by gallants courting their ladies (or prospecting for new ladies to court), and by thieves, pickpockets and traders. Tailors came there to study the latest in fashions, and around the north door gathered balladmongers, sellers of broadsides and street musicians.

We made our way through a confusion of people and their accompanying odors. People crowded about the stalls, listening to the pitch of the venders, or to the more intimate sounds of rustling petticoats.

Peter Tallis proved to be a man of middle age, with curled gray hair at his temples and no wig. When I stated my purpose he leaned back in his chair with a fat smile. "Hah! At last a new request! I have been asked for everything but this! Yet . . . it amuses me. And I know of these notes."

"You have seen them?"

"Ah, no! But . . . I knew the man. He came often

to the Walk to question people. As you know, this is the greatest clearing house for information in all of London—perhaps the greatest in Europe. More business is done here in a day than at the Royal Exchange in a week.

"You wish a copy of *all* his notes? I have the very man for it . . . a student. Very bright, very sharp." He glanced up at me again. "Who shall I say wants this work?"

"You need not say. Had I the time I would find and copy the notes myself, but I need them now. At once."

"You can write?" Tallis was skeptical.

"As well as you, my friend, and perhaps better," I replied brusquely. "When the copy of the book is ready I shall pay you eight shillings for it."

"It is very little."

"It is very much. A farm laborer makes but three shillings a week."

"This is a man who can write," Tallis protested. "Ten shillings."

"Nine, then," I said, "but not a penny more, or I do it myself."

"Nine then." He paused. "Where shall it be delivered?"

"I will come back in one week," I said.

"Nine shillings!" Jublain protested, as we walked away. "Are you made of money? Nine shillings for something you have never seen! What are you thinking of?"

"It's a gamble," I replied frankly. "I need friends, and aside from you I have none. I need money, and believe I see a way to get it."

"It had better work," Jublain replied grimly. "You are spending enough."

Much of the money I had brought was gone. More would be gone by the week's end, but I still had four gold pieces, ancient coins brought to Britain by some traveler or soldier.

By dint of much walking I priced coins in various shops, even bought two in a junk shop where they lay amid a lot of mixed stuff. One was of bronze, the other silver.

"Look you," Jublain protested, when once more we sat in the inn with tankards of ale before us, "Essex is in Ireland. He will need fighting men. We could——"

"I have naught against the Irish."

"How many wars are there, that you pick and choose?"

"Go to Essex if you wish. I shall go to America, a quick voyage and home again with riches."

"You tell me to go? We are friends, Barnabas. Anyway, I must see what comes of this madness."

"Enough for now. There is a play at the Globe. In my life I have seen but one play and that in an inn yard. This is about Julius Caesar."

"If you must go, carry a sword. There are roving gangs, and even inside the theater there is trouble. The last time I went, some idle son threw a beef bone that near broke my skull."

"If you have not heard," it was the man for whom I'd bought the meal, "you had best know. The theater sits now on the Bankside near Maiden Lane. They took it up one night and carried it over the Thames."

"Carried a theater? What nonsense is this?"

"The old man, Burbage, died and left the theater to his sons, Cuthbert and Richard. Left the building, that is. It stood upon land belonging to Alleyn, who would not lease it to them."

"So?"

"One dark night a set of rough fellows, Richard Burbage among them. came across the river armed with swords, daggers, bills and hooks. They tore down the theater and took it over the river. The Thames was frozen, so they carried it over on the ice.

"Alleyn was that beside himself, but he had not the men to stop them. Burbage had a carpenter named Streat with him, and William Smyth and who knows who else? Some say Will Kemp was along, and Shakespeare, too, that actor who writes."

"You seem to know a bit of all that goes on," I commented.

"Aye, if you've aught to sell, I will find a buyer. If there's a place you'd go, I can take you there. If there's a man you must meet, I can arrange that, too."

"And a woman?" Jublain suggested.

"That a man must do for himself, unless. . . ."

"Unless what?"

"If it were business, serious busines. . . ."

"And your name?"

"I am Corvino, once an acrobat and a clown."

"No longer?"

"I took a fall. I am agile enough, but not for that. Not again. Not me."

"Come with us to the theater, Corvino. I have a matter to discuss. There is a Society of Antiquaries. Do you know of them?"

"A bit."

The plan that had come to me was not complicated. In our Elizabethan world, to succeed a man needed at least strength, courage, and, if not those, the favor of friends. I was ambitious, I suppose, but I had no connections at court, nor was I wishful to enter that world. I wanted to do something, to accomplish, to achieve, but even for that one needed opportunity. And opportunity could be had only through the favor of some great man.

The discovery on the Devil's Dyke was an omen. It was a beginning, a foothold.

America promised much, or seemed to. A new world with furs, hides, perhaps even gold or pearls. If the Spanish had found them, why not the English?

Yet any move I might make required more capital than I had, and I had no wish to sell what my father had left me. The ancient coins had opened a way for me, had let me realize there were men who collected ancient things.

Hasling had accepted me; but Hasling was a rare man. Others would be more skeptical—hence the new clothes, the step into a world of fashion.

During my travels about to find work, or simply to look, I had come upon a ruined wall here, a bit of terrace there, a mound of earth, a grass-grown earthwork. And that section of mosaic I had glimpsed . . . a villa? Working men in England were constantly turning up some odd bit. I would not only use what I knew myself, but would study Leland's notes. If I could find something of value, I might realize the capital I'd need. Moreover, there was the chance of meeting some man of eminence who might speak to a ship's master for me.

I would not sit waiting for some vague tomorrow, nor for something to *happen*. One could wait a lifetime, and find nothing at the end of the waiting. I would begin here, I would make something happen.

"To the theater then," I said.

Chapter 5

Circumstance and heritage had produced a certain piece of raw material, the very raw material that was me. Yet, thanks to my father, my sophistication was beyond that of most fen-men.

To the theater we went, an oval, wooden-walled building with its center open to the sky, the galleries thatched. There were six-penny, two-penny, even penny seats, and if rain fell, it fell upon those in the pit—upon the sailors, mercers, butchers and bakers as well as their apprentices and students who occupied the pit.

There were also private theaters, but the audience for the plays of Will Shakespeare and many others was largely of the working-class and young.

Waiting for the play to begin, they argued boisterously, drinking beer, eating fruit or bread, cracking nuts.

We found a place in the balcony. From the pit somebody shouted a coarse remark at Jublain and he replied in kind. Next to us three young rowdies, albeit of good family, were throwing apple cores and nutshells on the heads below, and those in the pit threw them back.

At one side of the pit was an up-ended hogshead for the relief of those in the audience who had drunk more beer than they could handle. When the odor grew too great even for those in the pit, a cry went up to "Burn the juniper!"

After the call had come from several throats, an attendant appeared on stage with a metal plate and some twigs of juniper, which he set afire. Soon the pungent smell of burning juniper filled the air.

We watched the theater fill. "He's popular, Will Shakespeare is," Jublain informed us, "and they say *Julius Caesar* is one of his best."

It was little enough I knew of the theater, and nothing of Shakespeare. Of Fletcher and Marlowe I'd heard.

"The crowd likes him. He's been writing two plays a year, and playing parts in dozens of plays, his own and others. They usually change the bill twice each week. He's never played in the private theaters, although he has performed at court.

"Owns a part of the theater, Will does. When Burbage needed money to rebuild his theater on this side of the river he sold off parts of it to several of the actors. Shakespeare, Kemp, and three or four others put up money.

"But the crowd likes our Will. They understand what he says and like listening. He's one of the few who's had no trouble."

"Trouble?"

"They've smashed up some theaters, beaten up a few playwrights . . . actors, too. But not our Will."

Suddenly from behind me a harsh voice: "There he is! *Take him!*"

Turning swiftly, I saw Rupert Genester. A half-dozen hardfaced rogues were pushing up from behind him.

Corvino got up suddenly, stumbled and fell in front of them. Sprawling just in time to trip them, he gave

me the time I needed. Swinging over the rail in front
of the balcony, I lowered myself down, swung my
body once, then let go, dropping to the floor of the
balcony below. People shouted, a woman screamed,
then they scattered before me as I leaped for the rail
and dropped to the pit.

Above me I heard angry shouts, cursing, and then
I ducked through the door and outside.

It was totally dark. I ran a dozen steps, cut right
into a maze of alleyways, then turned abruptly right
again and emerged in a lane. Slowing my pace I
walked swiftly, listening for sounds of pursuit.

Only Corvino's timely fall, a very neat trick, had
saved me. Now where to go? Did they know I was
staying at the Tabard? That I doubted, but it would
not take them long to cover the town now it was
known that I was present.

Under trees near a barnyard, I paused, and wondered what to do. It was cold. Fresh patches of an
early snow still lay on the ground.

Yet the bold way was ever the right way for me,
and some distance away I saw the dark bulk of a
house of some size. It seemed to be a place of importance, with a number of outbuildings.

Walking along the lane, picking my way around
puddles of muddy water, I opened the gate at last.
Immediately, I was rushed by several huge dogs,
barking furiously.

Standing very still, I called out to the house. After
a moment, a chain rattled, I heard a bar removed,
and the door opened cautiously. A woman stood in
the door, candle in hand.

"Bruno! *Silence!*"

A woman certainly, and a young woman, I believed.
I spoke quietly, just loud enough to be heard. "Ma-

dam? Will you call off your dogs? I am in trouble enough, without this."

"Who are you?"

I walked toward her, the dogs snuffing at my legs, and one of them leaning rather hard against me. "An unfortunate traveler who has been attacked by ruffians."

It could not be an unfamiliar story. London had its share of scoundrels.

"I have escaped them, madam, but have no idea how far I am from London Bridge, or how I am to return."

By that time I had advanced into the light and my elegant but modest dress seemed to convince her. "Come. Please come in."

She stood aside, and hat in hand, I entered. Behind her stood a young woman, obviously a servant, but one of awesome dimensions. She looked upon me with no favor.

The other woman, a girl, who held the candle, was several years younger than I . . . and she was lovely.

"I fear I cause you inconvenience," I said. "If you will but show me the road——"

"You cannot walk the roads hereabouts at night," she said severely. "Lila, prepare a bed for this gentleman in the spare chamber."

Lila was about to protest, and at any other time I would have commended her good sense (and had it been any other than myself), but before she could speak her objections, the young lady spoke again, an edge to her tone. "Lila! I believe you heard me."

With a flounce, Lila turned and went away, every inch of her body stiff with disapproval.

The young lady led the way into a large, square room furnished in the heavy style of a few years back.

"Would you have a bit of something? If my father were here I am sure he would offer you something. Some sack, perhaps?"

Reflecting that I had chanced into a fortunate situation, I said, "Please."

She filled a small glass, then stood back.

"None for yourself?"

"Oh, no, sir! I never touch it!"

The "sir" was rather more than I was entitled to, yet I was suddenly wary. After all, what did I know of this place? Perhaps I had stumbled into a den of murderers.

A second look convinced me I was a fool. This was a very young girl, gently bred, her cheeks soft, no hint of hardness. And I had my sword.

"I am Barnabas Sackett, at your service!"

"I am Abigail Tempany."

Ignorant as I was of London and its people, I had heard the name only the day before. Her grandfather had a young son who amassed a fortune trading in Venice, Constantinople and the Black Sea. Only recently he had returned to his English lands, beginning at once to outfit ships for the New World. Aware of all such talk because of my own plans, the name had struck me as one to whom I might hope to speak.

We talked for a short time while I enjoyed the sack, purposely prolonging it because of my pleasure in her company. She knew little of London, and I must have seemed very knowing with all my easy talk of Jonson, Marlowe, Shakespeare and Will Kemp, much of which I had only heard that evening.

She bade me good-night, and Lila showed me to a chamber.

"I sleep lightly," Lila suggested warningly, and I smiled at her. "Very lightly," she added.

"And I, also," I said. "A trouble, is it not?"

Yet it seemed I had scarcely slept when morning was graying my window. I arose, bathed lightly and donned by clothes. I was hesitating to decide whether I should simply leave quietly or wait until I could pay my respects when there was a light tap on the door.

It was, of course, Lila.

"The master is breaking his fast. He requests your presence," she said.

Captain Brian Tempany was a stalwart, gray-haired man with a spade beard darker than his hair. He shot me a hard, level look from cool blue eyes and gestured to a seat.

"Ruffians, was it? Hadn't you a sword?"

"I had . . . and have. But there were a number of them and I became separated from my friends."

He looked at me coolly and waited until I was seated. "I was at the theater," he said bluntly, "in the box next to the one into which you dropped."

"I could not easily have explained all that," I said, embarrassed, "and might have frightened your daughter."

"Abigail," he said grimly, "is not easily frightened. She stood beside me off the Malabar coast and used a pistol to repel pirates who were attempting to board us."

He faced me squarely. "Why were you fleeing like a rogue from Rupert Genester?"

Lying would serve no purpose, and this man was no fool. As briefly as possible, I explained.

"Ivo's son, eh? I know the name. He was a fighting man. And you? What of you?"

"He taught me the blade, Captain."

"He did, did he? Well, probably it was better to

avoid them. A bunch of rascals, Genester included." He stared at me. "You wish to return to London?"

"I have a meeting there with the man I mentioned."

"To whom you would sell your coins? May I see them?"

From my purse, hidden inside my shirt, I took them out and placed them upon the table.

He touched them with his finger, studying them intently. "Yes, yes . . . good! Good!"

He stirred them about, studying the light as it fell upon the details of the coins. "I will buy them."

I was startled. "I had promised Coveney Hasling—"

"It will be well with him. As a matter of truth, I wish to make a gift of these coins to the very man to whom he planned to show them."

"You know him?"

"I do. England is a small country, after all. Men with like interests tend to know each other. I am not a member of the Society of Antiquaries, but I know of them. This man to whom Hasling would show the coins is a man of influence at court, where I need a word spoken for me."

"You say you know him?"

He smiled. "And he knows of you. This gentleman of the Antiquaries is the very man whom your father defended so nobly on the battlefield. The story is well known, Sackett.

"Not only was your father a very brave man and a tremendous fighter, but this Earl is a man who always appreciates what was done for him. Too many forget too readily, but he has made the story known everywhere. He is a man of great influence who could advance your career."

"I would enjoy that, but——"

"But what?"

"I understand you are sending a vessel to the New World. I would prefer to sail with her, Captain. I have it in mind to venture a small sum in goods."

"Venture? How much?"

"What those are worth, and a bit more. Hopefully, quite a bit more."

He laughed. Then he got to his feet and went to the sideboard for a bottle. "Here! Try a man's drink!"

"No," I said, "the ale will do."

His smile faded. He was not a man accustomed to refusal. Then he shrugged. "Fine . . . so be it."

When our glasses were filled he sat down again. "All right, buy your goods. I shall have a ship sailing within a fortnight, and you shall go with her."

"And two friends?"

"Are they fighting men?"

"They are."

"Then go they shall, Sackett. Go they shall."

I stood up and he shook my hand. It was not until I was astride one of his horses and on my way to London that I began to worry.

It was all working out too well, much too well. And that bothered me.

As I approached London Bridge, I loosened my sword in its scabbard.

Chapter 6

Approaching the Tabard I drew up and carefully observed for several minutes. There seemed no one about who should not be there, so I rode into the yard.

Jublain came out from the taproom followed by Corvino. "Ah? You've the devil's own luck! You got clean away!"

"Thanks to Corvino's tumble. Has there been anyone about?"

"Had there been we would have been awaiting you down the street, one of us each way and ready with a warning." Jublain glanced at the horse. "Where did you steal it?"

"It was borrowed from a gentleman whose man will pick it up later. Not only that," I said as I dismounted, "but I've passage for us, a trading venture to the Americas in a Tempany ship."

"You're a lucky one," Jublain grumbled, "but I fear for you. It goes too well."

That I felt the same I did not say. "Perhaps. But we will purchase our goods and be ready for the sailing."

Lying abed that night and before sleep claimed me, I considered my situation. There was a book newly published by Richard Hakluyt, and in it he was said to tell of voyages to America. I would have that book, and what charts could be found, though realizing the charts might be of doubtful value.

I also thought upon the tile floor I had come upon not too far from London. Several of my discoveries of such places had come while working, and few of us paid attention to what was found underground. My own curiosity and my father's comments had alerted me, however, but this particular find was not on a job.

The day was late and I had walked far and was eagerly seeking shelter from the night—some hut, perhaps an inn, even a ruin, when I heard horses coming up behind me.

Encountering other travelers on the road late at night was not always to be welcomed, so I stepped back into the trees and brush and made myself small behind the thick trunk of an oak.

The two men who rode up the road were far from the sort I wished to encounter, but they rode past. When I started to come from behind my tree, something gave way under foot and I slid a few feet. Catching at a branch I managed to hold myself, and then to steady my feet.

I listened, but the riders were gone. Turning, I peered into the dark, could see nothing. Taking a stone from the ground, I prepared to toss it into the blackness to see if there was indeed a pit or a hole there, when my fingers told me that what I held was not the texture of a stone but more in the nature of a piece of tile, a bit of mosaic, perhaps.

Crouching down, I felt with my hands and found the place where my feet had slid. I tossed a bit of branch in that direction. It seemed to fall only a few feet. Feeling around, I found an edge of tile flooring projecting from the mud at least three feet below the surrounding level.

My decision was instant. I would go no further

47

that night. I could barely make out a small hollow below the projection of tile. Feeling my way into it I gathered fuel and built a small, carefully sheltered fire. There I waited until daybreak, making a small meal of cheese and bread.

Fitfully, I slept. When day came at last I found myself in a small hollow. The tile flooring was above me, and the place where I had slept was open to the sky, except for a few branches spreading above it.

Prodding around with my stick I came up with more broken tile, some odds and ends of pottery fragments, and a piece of broken statue: the severed part of a hand.

It was to this place I wanted to return. There was every chance that I might find there some things of value.

The next day I went early to the common room. With ale before me, I listened to the idle gossip. Luke Hutton, the highwayman, had been hung by his neck in York, some months past, but there was still talk as to who he actually was. He had been a scholar at Cambridge, and some even said he was a son of the Archbishop of York.

There was talk of recruiting for the wars in Ireland, and of the fighting there. But Essex had not yet gone over, waiting, it was said, for provisions.

Meanwhile, talking with divers persons, I bargained for items I would take to the New World. Beads of glass and sharp knives, needles, bolts of highly colored cloth. I wished not to be heavily loaded, to have only what was necessary. I talked with men who knew about sailing westward, and there were a few who had traded across the Atlantic for many years.

One was a man from Bristol who scoffed at the "discovery" of the New World. "Our people have been fishing off the Banks for many years. We often landed on New Found Land, or the mainland shores, to dry fish or smoke them. But it was a harsh and savage land and who cared about it? We saw no gold. We saw only rocky coasts or long sandy shores with forest behind them."

It was exciting to listen to such men, and to hear the news. A witch named Doll Barthram had been hanged in Suffolk. We had heard talk of her even back in the fens.

Twice there were meetings with Captain Tempany. He listened to my list of purchases, added a suggestion or two, then commented, "We've little time. There's a ship's captain newly come to Plymouth who says the King of Spain will soon send a great fleet against us. We must be well out to sea before they come, or we'll be taken."

"Is your ship not armed?"

"Armed? Aye, she's armed, but what can six guns do against a fleet? No, no. I would prefer to slip down the river in the dark. There's nought to be gained by fighting, for even if we 'scaped we'd likely take a shot through the rigging or hull. Stand by now, for word will come quickly and move we shall, on the instant."

Tempany hesitated, rubbing his jaw. "There's another thing. You've heard of Nick Bardle?"

"A hard man, they say."

"Aye. A thief and a pirate, and whatever is evil and wrong. Well, he's moored close by my ship and I like none of it. He's a man will bear watching. Mind you, he'd think twice before troubling me, unless he could steal a bit of my cargo and make a run for it."

He drummed on the table with his fingers. "Know you aught of America?"

"I've read Hakluyt, and I've heard talk."

"You know more than most. The Spanish have settled in what they call Floridy. There were some French, but I think they've been driven out or killed by the Spanish. Raleigh settled some colonists with a man named Lane to head them, but they came back, first chance. Grenville left fifteen men . . . all vanished. Killed by Indians or Spaniards, no doubt."

"Or picked up and gone elsewhere."

"The Indians . . . well, you must be wary of them, lad. Today they will trade, and tomorrow if the notion takes them, they attack. If one gives you his word, it counts for something. But he speaks only for his own people.

"They've no sense of property. Not as we have. In a village each man uses what he needs. When they see something they want, they take it and go.

"Above all, go with no notions about gold. The Spanish found it in Mexico, but the French have not found it anywhere. The gold is to be had in the trading for furs, skins, freshwater pearls, fish and potash. Some of their hardwoods burn with a fine white ash, and there's a need for potash."

"What should I deal in?"

"Furs. You've only a little stake, so trade with care. Only furs, and only the best. Take second-grade furs and that's all you will ever get. The Indians are not fools. They've lived by barter all their lives, and they know what they want."

"A handful of beads for a fox-skin does not seem a very good trade for them."

"Ah, lad! He has plenty of fox-skins, but he has no beads such as ours. The scarcer the article the greater the value. You pay for what you want; so does the Indian.

"Good knives, they have need of them. They'll try for muskets, too, but do not be trading them. Arm them as well as us and they would soon have everything."

"They'd rob us?"

"Of course, and so would a Dunkirker. Trust no ship at sea, lad. Given a chance there's few of them will not turn pirate . . . or privateer, or whatever you wish to call them."

He motioned for a refill of our tankards. "We shall sail south, almost to the land of the Spanish men, then north along the coast, trading wherever possible. After that, to some islands off the north coast where fishermen have summer villages to dry and smoke their fish. There we'll refit and buy stores."

Tempany hoisted his glass, looking from under bushy gray brows at me. "Lad, have you thought there's more to Genester's hatred of you than what happened in Stamford?"

"Why should there be? We never met before."

"Agreed. Nor had he seen you or known of you, but think you now: once his anger was gone, would he have bothered unless there was something more?"

"Impossible, Captain. He has wealth, position, all a man could ask. I have nothing but a will to do."

"Suppose you were a threat to his keeping what he has? Or gaining more?"

"There is no way, Captain. To him I was just an oaf, a country bumpkin whom he believed to be making overtures to his lady."

"Until his anger led him to discover who you were."

"I am Barnabas Sackett, no more. I am a man of the

fens, who, because his father was a skilled fighting man, holds a bit of land."

"And to whose father a promise was made."

"Oh? That! Captain, if indeed such a word was passed, it meant only that he might see me in some post where I could have a living."

"I agree that was the intention, lad, but things have happened. This man . . . he will disclose his name when he sees fit . . . lost a son when the Armada attacked. He lost a son in the plague. Suddenly he is no longer young, and finds as his only heir a man, a nephew whom he profoundly dislikes."

"Genester?"

"Aye." Tempany took a swallow of the ale and touched his beard with the back of his hand. "A night came when he was sitting about talking of antiquities, and one of the old friends shows two gold coins and tells their tale.

"Suddenly, the elderly gentleman of whom I speak is hearing again the name of that stalwart who stood above him and fought off the attackers until help came.

"He recalls the stern, honest quality of that man, and now he hears of that man's son. A promise is recalled, and Hasling comments on your enterprise in coming to him, your knowledge of antiquities . . . which he probably overrated . . . and your difficulties with Genester."

"Still, I do not——"

Tempany lifted a hand. "Wait. Hasling had his story to tell, and then I told mine, of the affair at the Globe and returning to find you at my home.

"The gentleman of whom I speak decided the fates were guiding him to a decision. He enjoyed the way you escaped so handily. It indicated presence of mind, and your dumping of Genester on your first meeting brought him to chuckling and wishing he could have seen it."

"I had a good friend who impeded pursuit. Do not forget that, Captain. But for Corvino——"

"Having such friends is a credit to you. I do not jest, lad. He wishes to meet you."

"It would be a pleasure, Captain."

"Aye, but somehow Genester has discovered that. Perhaps from one of the servants. I do not know. Genester's hopes center around the old man. He himself has little, so if the old man should choose to leave his estates to you——"

"That is impossible, Captain."

"No, not at all. It presents the solution to a problem. He respected your father, and you have shown yourself to be a young man of wit, intelligence and decision, something he was himself, and which he admires. So, before you go further with this trading venture, talk to him."

"I shall, of course, but I would choose to make my own way, Captain. How many of the titled gentlemen around the Queen have done as much? Raleigh, perhaps."

"As you will, but meet with him, at least. I shall see him soon. In the meanwhile, be careful."

The interest of great men is flattering, but I had no faith in such matters. I had found no luck and no opportunity except that I made. Finding the gold— that was luck, but on the other hand, had I not been walking the Dyke home from work I would never have been where the gold was. It did not come to me. I went to it.

"I shall be out of the way for two, maybe three days," I suggested.

He glanced at me, and I said, "It is a venture in antiquities, and may come to nothing."

"Luck to you, then. Be in touch with me when you return. I will arrange the meeting for then."

When he had gone, I met with Jublain and Corvino. "I shall need a horse," I said.

"A horse is easy," Corvino said. "Why not three?"

"What I do may come to nothing."

Jublain shrugged. "Much of what any of us do comes to nothing, yet I notice that whatever you do has at least an intelligence."

Quietly, I explained. "Do not think of treasure," I warned. "It may be some simple thing. A pot, a Roman sword, an inscription. We may waste our time."

"If you go alone," Jublain said, "you'll fall into trouble. We shall ride with you."

We took only the food we needed, and digging tools. The latter we wrapped in a cloak and we rode swiftly. Out of town and long into the countryside, then into the deep woods.

Suddenly Jublain said, "We are followed, Barnabas."

Glancing back I saw a lone horseman upon a hill. He was sitting very still, seeming to scan the country.

"Just a chance rider," I suggested.

"Who turns when we turn? Who stops when we stop?"

"All right then, be prepared."

Our horses were good, but I had no mind to trust to speed. I had walked through this country before this. The road ahead dipped low between a barn and a walled field. Beyond was a sunken road, a road that branched three ways. Between two of these roads was a brook.

Swiftly we dipped into the sunken road. We took the middle one and, coming to the brook, went into the water and rode swiftly to the other road and into the woods. Turning from the road we rode into the forest, weaving among the trees, splashing through a marsh and soon came upon another trail.

We went back, then, by devious lanes used only by farmers, into the deeper forest.

Though I was sure I could ride right to the spot, it took me some time to find it. We dismounted and looked about. It was Corvino whose quick eyes made contact.

"There!" he said. "Where the mound is! That is probably all tumbled rock underneath. See? It is not a natural mound, that one."

Jublain had not moved. Suddenly he looked over at me. "It is wrong . . . this," he said quietly. "It is very wrong."

We looked at him, and he flushed a little. "You'll think me a fool," he said, "but if there is anything here, if there are old things, they lie as they have fallen . . . where they fell, when they fell."

Neither of us knew what he was talking about. "Is it because you fear the ghosts?" Corvino wondered.

Jublain shook his head. "I know nothing of such things," he said, "I should be the last to speak, but your Society. . . . If this place were opened with care, if every thing were taken out and its position marked, could one not tell how the object was used? You spoke of pots . . . for the kitchen? Or for perfumes or powder or such things? If things are moved, how will they ever find out?"

We stared at him, and I, for one, saw his point at last. It irritated me, because I began to feel he was right. I did not know exactly why, but . . .

"You spoke of history, of these things being a

part of history. If we take them all apart, then who will know how they once fitted?"

"If *we* don't, someone else will," I grumbled.

"I think that remark has excused more sins than any other," Jublain commented.

I stared at him, irritated. "Since when did you become so sanctimonious? You have killed, looted. You've lived by the sword."

He shrugged. "A good point, and I'm caught upon it. I am a soldier, have on occasion been a brigand, but nonetheless——"

"Dig!" I said, "I came not this way for nothing."

Corvino had crossed the hollow where I had fallen on my first discovery. "A corner was here, I think. Let us try."

Nobody said more, and we all dug, but reluctantly, I think.

We found broken stone, another fragment of a statue, a bit of a robe this time, much dirt and debris, more fallen rock and finally a whole wall that had fallen in. Then much finer soil, dust that had blown in, the black soil of moldered leaves, some fragments of broken pottery.

They worked slowly, and with great care, breaking up each clod of mud, searching for whatever they might find. Jublain straightened at last. "Barnabas," he said, "there is something here. The floor," he pointed up, "is there. What we find here is under the floor."

"A cellar. A tunnel, perhaps," I suggested.

Corvino shook his head. "I think not. The place of the floor was built above this, built after it. What we are working now is the edge of an older ruin . . . before the Romans."

"Who was here before the Romans?" Jublain asked.

I shrugged. "Arthur . . . you have heard of him? Arthur was here. He was a Celt, I think. And the Danes were here, they came and went. My own people were among those who were here. But . . . who knows?"

We hesitated. I looked up at the floor, about five feet above where we now worked. "It may be for nothing, for no purpose," I said irritably.

Jublain leaned on his shovel. "We should leave it alone," he insisted. "We know nothing of this. Perhaps if your antiquaries came here to dig——"

"They might know little more," I said. "Jublain, work on the floor above. Corvino and I will work down here. We will disturb as little as possible."

Suddenly a thought came to me. That rider who seemed to follow us: what of him?

"Keep your weapons close," I said suddenly. "I have a bad feeling about this place."

"Aye," Jublain was grim. "Men have died here. See?" He indicated some charred and ancient timber he had uncovered. "Fire . . . and blood, I am thinking."

Corvino dug carefully in the corner, removing the dirt bit by bit.

I watched, then returned to my own digging. The earth was black and rich . . . with the bodies of the dead? Who had lived and died in this place? Did they believe their world was all? Did they look with amused interest mingled with mild contempt at the past?

Something rounded and smooth . . . something! "A skull," I said, removing it gently from the soil, "a skull cleft by a blow."

There it was, the bone parted from behind by a blow. I took it up, gently. Placing it at one side I

57

slowly worked about, finding other bones, scattered finger bones, a pelvis . . . suddenly some metal studs from a belt or something, and then a small packet of coins. They were stuck together, but I lifted them out. There must have been a dozen, most of them gold. Two came free as I lifted them.

One had a horse with its head looking back, tail flowing, and what might have been a chariot behind. There was a worn figure, man or woman we could not tell. Another was of a seated woman, holding a staff, and some symbols or letters behind the staff.

"There!" Jublain indicated them. "We have found what we came for. Let us go."

"You? The looter? You wish to leave now?" I scoffed gently.

"It is you who have done this to me," he said calmly. "You with your talk of preserving history. I had not thought of it before, but what do we who make history have left, if our victories and defeats are not known to our ancestors?

"I think . . . I feel some lonely battle was fought here, and fought well, and men died for what they believed, perhaps surrounded in this place. Someday men may come with more knowledge than we and they will put the parts together. And out of it will come a story of heroes."

"You believe in heroes?" Corvino looked at him thoughtfully.

"I cannot believe in anything else. A man needs heroes. He needs to believe in strength, nobility and courage. Otherwise we become sheep to be herded to the slaughterhouse of death. I believe this. I am a soldier. I try to fight for the right cause. Sometimes it is hard to know.

"But I do not sit back and sneer in cowardice at

those with the courage to fight. The blood of good men makes the earth rich, as it is here. When I die sword in hand, I hope someone lives to sing of it. I live my life so that when death comes I may die well. I ask no more."

"We will go," I said.

The coins I put away. We climbed from the hole and brushed away the dirt of our digging. Then, remembering what Jublain had said, I kicked with my heels at the edge and caved the earth into the hole. Then I threw in some broken branches and a few stones that lay about.

"Let us go to our horses," I said. "We can ride a little way before dark."

Together we walked back through the darkening forest, not talking, each alive with his own thinking. And so we came to the small clearing where our horses were, and they awaited us there. Eight men with swords. In my present mood, it was not too many.

I threw my shovel into their faces and went in with my sword. Staggered or leaping to escape the flying shovel, they were momentarily taken aback, and my swinging laid open the cheek of one man, scarred the brow of the man next to him. Both were bloody in an instant, and I was parrying a blow from another.

Jublain had been no less swift. Accustomed to attack and counterattack, he had gone in low and fast. One who had leaped back from the shovel had thrown his hands high, and Jublain's point parted his laces down the middle of his stomach. The blade went in— I seemed to see it go. Then he was cutting left with it.

Suddenly the attack was over and they were gone. Corvino had scooped a handful of earth and flung it into their eyes, and brought down two with the flat of his shovel.

"They've gone?" I looked about me. Two men were down, one moaning softly, one completely unconscious. The others were staggering as they fled.

"Hired men like them are cowards!" Jublain said contemptuously. "They are not fighting men. They'd steal a purse from an old woman, or three or four might attack someone. They are only vicious, and have neither courage nor the heart for a fight."

Nonetheless, we had taken some bruises. A point had cut my sleeve, scratching my arm, and Corvino had a bad bruise where a cudgel had struck him on the shoulder.

We mounted, the richer by two swords and a dagger, dropped and left behind. The wounded we left where they were, to get back as best they might.

"We must leave the Tabard," I said, as we rode back. "If they do not know we are there, they will find us."

"Where then?" Jublain asked.

"There is a place," Corvino said, "kept by a sailor's wife. It is clean, well-kept. I have stayed there."

"And there's the ship," I said, "we can go aboard her."

Yet we had left some few things at the Tabard, and went back for them. Coveney Hasling was in the common room when we entered.

"Ah? You have returned," he greeted me.

"I have some things," I said.

Taking our ale with us, we climbed to our room on the floor above. There I opened the packet and showed him, explaining the find.

"Excellent!" He pinched his nose with two fingers as he studied them one by one. "Truly excellent. This packet, as is, will bring a pretty price. As for the coins——"

"Do take them then," I said, "and do the best you can. Pay the money, when you get it, to my account with Captain Tempany, and I'll be obliged."

Pushing the packet to Hasling, I said, "Jublain, you and Corvino take our goods to the Tempany ship. It is the *Tiger* . . . a three-master of two hundred tons, no forecastle. Take our goods aboard and await me there. I must go to Saint Paul's Walk."

"Do you be careful, then," Jublain said. "It is a place where anything might happen."

"Genester will not yet have the news of what happened, I think. Those who fail are not swift to report their failure. I shall go, then come on board with the remainder of our goods."

"Our goods?" Jublain stared at me. "Yours, rather."

"Ours," I said, "one-half for me, one-quarter each for you. If either of you decides to leave, you leave your goods as well."

Corvino smiled. "It is more than I ever had, this lot," he said. "And I shall stay with you, Master Sackett."

"I, also," Jublain said. "One way or the other I am like to get a cracked skull. It is better in company that I like."

Saint Paul's Walk was crowded as ever, yet I found my way to Peter Tallis's stall. He smiled up at me, and thrust a packet of manuscript to me. "There it is," he said, "ready and waiting."

I ran through the lot, scanning a page here and there. It was, indeed, what I wanted. I paid the sum.

Tallis smiled at me as he took it. "If you've further need for such things," he said, "I can put a hand upon them. I like your business. It is different."

"We will talk, then." I sat down on a bench. "You may be able to help me more."

He indicated the sheaf of manuscript. "Most of what I do is dull stuff. This I enjoyed. I read it. Now I know more of England than else I should ever have known."

"It is said," I began, "there are charts to be had of the New World. Charts even the Admirals know nothing of."

"Charts?" His eyes wrinkled at the corners. "Yes, yes, of course. It is a quiet pleasure of mine, this matter of charts. Richard Hakluyt has come to me from time to time, but he wants the accounts more than the charts, and also——"

"Also?"

"He has too many friends who are men of power. I sometimes come upon things it would be difficult to explain. But to you . . . ?"

"To me? I would say nothing of the source. Talk to me of charts."

He stood up to gather his gear together. "I will close the booth. There is a tavern close by. I think we will talk better there."

Peter Tallis was no common man but a scholar in his way, a shrewd man with not too many scruples but more than enough interest in my trade. Over ale in the shadows of a small place nearby we talked. Finally, it was agreed. For a fitting sum, he removed from his bundle and gave me a dozen charts.

We talked of many things, and the hour grew late. Finally, my roll of charts beneath my arm, I returned to the Tabard. All was quiet. Only one man loafed about, a dark, sullen-looking fellow with a wet look to his eyes I did not like. He lurked near a cart, and I asked him if it was his, and for hire. To both questions he agreed.

With his help I loaded the rest of my goods into the cart, including in one of the bags the charts I had obtained.

"I want to go to the *Tiger*. Do you know the ship?"

"Tempany's vessel? I know it."

It took us several trips. A soft rain was falling by the time we last were loaded. Hunched in my heavy cloak, I walked behind the cart, whose wheels rumbled over the cobbles.

I saw the spars of the *Tiger* looming ahead. Beside it the La Rochelle pinnace that was Nick Bardle's ship, the *Jolly Jack*.

Tired as I was, and sleepy, I thought only of the warm bunk awaiting me aboard the *Tiger*. I glanced at Bardle's ship, all dark and still, yawned, then heard a rush of feet behind me.

Turning swiftly, my hand went to my sword hilt, but my heavy cloak got in the way, and the carter suddenly jostled me off-balance. They closed in on me from all sides. I struggled, but my arms were pinned to my side, a cloak thrown over my head and jerked tight around me, my cries muffled. A blow on the head caused me to fall. I started to rise, saw the futility of it. For if I tried again, they might kill me there. If I lay quiet, they might think me worse off than I was.

A voice said, "Well done!" I heard a clink of coins from hand to hand. "Remember, Bardle, I never want to see or hear of him again!"

"No need to fret. There's a sight of deep water betwixt here and America!"

Chapter 7

Rough hands took me up and I was carried aboard and dropped through a hatch to the cargo. My goods were dumped in after me, and the hatch was battened down. It was close and hot in the hold.

When the hatch was closed I tried to sit up but my head spun and pain throbbed dizzily in my skull. I managed to free my body from the cloak. I lay back, breathing heavily in the close, hot air. I had been hit harder than I realized, a mild concussion. After a bit my consciousness slipped away and there was a long time when I was unaware of anything.

It was the movement that brought me alive, movement of a ship on the water. We must have come down the river during the night for there was more than river in the movement I felt. I sat up groggily, choking with thirst.

It was totally black in the hold, and when I tried to stand my head bumped the edge of the hatch.

There was a pounding of feet on the deck, shouting, and the creak of timbers. The ship began to move faster. I could feel it, I thought! I sat down, holding my head in my hands. They had me then, Nick Bardle, at Rupert Genester's orders.

Well, they wouldn't keep me. What was it he had said: there's a lot of deep water? We'd see about that.

I shook my head, and pain shot through me. No matter. I would have to be ready. I had no wish to die, to let such a scoundrel win.

What had they said of Bardle? That if he was shorthanded he would grab some country lad? Well, he had me. I doubted he would kill me when there was work to be had from me. And I was strong. In the quarries they had said I was strong as any two men. Yet I knew I was even stronger.

No matter what happened, I must get them to keep me alive and working. Then I could watch my chance. Nick Bardle would be no fool; he would know most of the dodges. Best not to fight unless they tried to kill me, not resist, not argue. Hold myself tight, and wait.

Again I slept, and when I opened my eyes it was to the deeper roll of the open sea. Scarcely had they opened when the hatch covers were lifted and a head thrust over the combing. "All right! Up with you! There's work to be done!"

I jumped up, caught the edge of the hatch and swung to the deck.

The mate drew back. He was a stocky, redheaded, red-faced man with a deep scar over his right eye. His small blue eyes were hard and mean. He was expecting trouble, and he had two stalwart men behind him . . . tough men by the looks of them.

"A ship!" I said. "Well, cursed I am if I am not on a ship! This is what I'd hoped for, to find a ship and get to sea!"

They were surprised. They stared. They had expected anger, protests, shouts, and trouble. Here I was, grinning at them.

"Will you show me how to be a sailor? All my life, I've wanted to go to sea!"

"We'll show you, all right!" The mate hadn't decided whether to be pleased or disappointed. "Get for'rd!"

Quickly, I obeyed, and when the hands turned to hoist the fores'l, I was in a hurry to help.

The hatch lay open, and I was scared. What if they examined my goods? But they did not. After awhile, the hatch was battened again.

It went against my grain to take the pushing I took, and no Sackett I ever heard of had stood for such action. Yet when I looked about me at the rest of the crew, I could see they were a bad lot, and no help would I get from them.

Anyway, that would be mutiny. Only it had to be mutiny, or something like it.

Now I made like I knew nothing about a ship, but I did. We in the fens often sailed out to sea. Wanting to make them feel they'd like to keep me alive, I buckled to and worked hard enough for two men.

By the third day I heard the mate, whose name was Berryman, tell Cap'n Bardle. "Don't you be hasty, Cap'n. That Sackett is worth two of any man aboard. He's got to be soft in the head, all he talks about is how he always wanted to be a sailorman. But he works like the devil and he's handy."

Bardle watched me then, whenever he was on deck. Several times he and Berryman talked, and one time Berryman asked, "You was a farmer ashore?"

"In the fens. We used boats a lot."

That seemed to satisfy them for awhile, but finally Berryman came to me again. "How'd a farmer like you get enemies?"

Now I had my chance, and I took it. I wanted them to have reason to keep me alive. "There's some that wanted me dead," I agreed, "but there's others who'd pay twice as much to keep me alive."

Nick Bardle had all he was likely to get from Rupert Genester, but here was another thought: there might be more to be made.

"That don't foller," Berryman commented, after a moment or two. "Who'd want you alive?"

"Now think." I said. "if a man will pay to have me dead, it's because he stands to profit by it. Just as he will profit if I die, there's others will lose, and those others want me alive.

"The man who wants me dead hasn't much. In fact, if I get back alive, he hasn't anything."

For two weeks then, all went well. I worked hard. They avoided me, but they made no effort to push me into dangerous jobs. Yet I trusted none of them. They were thieves and murderers, and I knew my time was short. They would mull it over, and they would decide if I had to die. There was too much chance of what I'd do to them if I somehow got back to England.

The weather held good. I kept an eye out for a distant sail, expecting Captain Tempany to be coming along soon, but I doubted he would want to overhaul the *Jolly Jack*. She had twelve guns that were heavier than those I'd seen on the *Tiger*. Moreover, the *Jack* clearly had a crew of pirates, or the next thing to them.

Then we came upon a spell of bad weather, with the wind set contrary, and made a bad time of it, day after day. Tempers grew short, and as best I could, I kept from the gaze of Berryman or Bardle, knowing I was the likely scapegoat. We sighted a sail once, then, on the fifth day of bad weather. But it was some distance off and where it sailed there was wind, as we could see the sails filled and the wind ruffling the water.

There was a man aboard to whom I found some liking—a brawny young man, strong yet not tall, a man of dark skin, yet not a Negro. He was a Moor, he told me, but I knew aught of Moors. He said a Moor was a man of Arab blood born in Africa, in the north of Africa where there were few blacks except slaves . . . and as many white slaves as black. His name was Sakim.

He was a good man at sea, and an able one. He had watched me from time to time but had said nothing until on this fifth day when we watched the far-off sail, he spoke softly, "No matter who she is, I'd prefer it to this."

"And I," I replied, with candor.

After a moment I said, "Are there others who feel so?"

"There's one," he said, "the Neapolitan, Rufisco."

He, too, had I seen; a small, agile man who reminded me of Corvino. It was something in their movements, their manner.

"Something might be done," I said, "if you've a mind to chance it."

"At sea?" he stared at me doubtfully.

"Near the shore." I said. "There's a coast off the mainland yonder."

"And savages?" he suggested.

"Better a risk of what we do not know than what we know. They do not intend me to return," I added. "I have nothing to lose. But you?"

"Nothing," he said. "I will speak to Rufisco."

There was hard work then, trimming sail with a squall coming up, and the wind ruffling the water in our direction. Our craft heeled far over under the blast, righted and put her bows down and went to it. She was a good sailer, that *Jolly Jack*, and belied her owners.

Nothing had come of my words with Sakim, but at least he seemed to keep them quiet.

We finally caught a decent wind and turned to the southwest with occasional squalls of rain but always some wind. And then, on the sixty-seventh day out, we sighted land again. It was afar off, and not to be made out, but Bardle simply gave our craft a little more southing and ignored the land.

In the middle of the night watch, the Moor came close. "Rufisco will chance it ashore.."

"The first time then. There may not be another."

"They will kill us," he said.

"My friend," I said quietly, "this rascal owes me, and when we go ashore, I'll have what belongs to me and whatever the passage was worth. Some damages, too."

"I like a confident man," Sakim said dryly. "Especially if he lives."

"I shall," I said. "At least to get a foot on shore."

Berryman hove up alongside. "Belay that!" he growled. "We have no time for gamming here. Be about your work."

"Aye," I said agreeably. "There's a bit to do."

Our watch ended and I went below, but not to sleep. I lay quiet until the others snored and then slipped from my bunk and to the sail locker. Crawling over the sails I found what I had seen before, a loose board that opened into the hold.

No doubt some sailor had arranged it so for pilfering a bit of cargo, but I had no wish for aught but my due, and I went through and into the dark hold. It took me a time longer than I wished to find my own things, but once there I opened a bale and felt about within.

Two pistols, powder and shot. A dozen loads for each. Three cutlasses of the four I'd brought along, and a fowling piece which I charged with shot as soon as I'd come back to the light of the sail locker.

Keeping one pistol in hand, I tucked the other in my belt. My own good blade had been taken by the captain when I came aboard, but I'd see to that. In the meantime the cutlasses were excellent weapons.

No man saw me move across the dark, wet deck. No man saw me re-enter the sleeping quarters. I shook awake Sakim and Rufisco and handed each a cutlass.

"Come!" I whispered. "This night we take a ship!"

We went out upon the deck and I pointed to a swivel gun on the bulwark. "Charge it," I said, "and when given the word, choose your best target."

Darkling was at the helm, a man for whom I'd no liking at all. As I came along the deck toward him, he saw me. "What er you a-doin' on deck?"

"Taking a ship," I said. "Put your wheel over four degrees."

"I'll do no such thing," he said.

I aimed the fowling piece at his belt buckle.

"Have it your way," I said. "The next man can do it standing over your body."

He eyed me a moment, sullen and furious, but he put the wheel over as I watched him. The wind was right, and we moved in toward the coast. I was sure there would be an action resulting, and there was. Berryman burst out upon the deck.

"What——?"

"Lie down on the hatch," I said.

He looked at me, and at the fowling piece and at

the pistols in my belt. He was a thinking man and he did as suggested.

"You," I said to Rufisco, "take the wheel and keep her in toward the coast. Darkling," I said, "lie down beside Berryman. With this fowling piece I can take two as well as one, be they close together."

All was still. Our speed was not great, but we were not far offshore. Until I had seen that dark finger of land, it had been no part of my plan to move so soon. There was on my chart a place such as that, and south of it some long, sandy islets. If I had been fortunate, if I had guessed right—for it was only a guess—those islands would be showing up.

"You're a great fool!" Berryman shouted from the deck. "You will swing for this!"

"When I tell all I know," I said pleasantly, "you will all swing."

The shore was nearing. I could smell it, and I could hear the surf upon the shore. We were moving on an oblique course but I had no intention of putting the ship aground, for to endanger the others was no part of my plan. They were rascals, no question of that, and a dirty, poisonous lot, enough to kill the fish for miles if dumped into the water.

We were moving slowly, making barely enough speed for proper handling. I went aft and pulled in the gig we had been towing astern.

My mouth was dry and I was scared, yet saw no alternative to what I intended. Darkling had started to rise when I turned the gun on him again. He slid back down and lay still.

"Nick will come," he threatened, "then you'll see!"

"Sakim," I said, "get the top off that hatch."

They had no idea what I intended, Berryman and Darkling, and, as they were ordered off the hatch, must have been wondering hard. With a sign I motioned Rufisco to put the lashings on the wheel, then to go forward and cut loose the anchor.

With Sakim holding the fowling piece, I went down into the hatch and retrieved my merchandise. Pulling the gig close in alongside, I lowered my gear into it. Working swiftly then, we bound and gagged Berryman and Darkling, then got into the ship's stores, taking out ship's biscuit, salt meat and a side of beef the captain had in keeping for himself.

"Stand by," I told them, "and keep a wary eye. I shall speak to the captain."

"What?" Rufisco stared at me. "He sleeps with a loaded pistol by him."

"Then he had better be quick with it," I said, "for I've a matter to discuss with him."

I went along aft, down the ladder's three steps to the after cabin, and there he lay, sprawled on his bunk with an empty bottle by him and the smell of rum strong upon the air. My sword lay across the room and I walked over and took it up.

He had a pistol by him, all right, but I took it rudely from under his hand. Then I nudged him a toe.

"Come alive," I said. "You've to settle accounts now."

He stirred, opened his eyes, then seeming to sense the stillness of the ship he suddenly woke up, threw back the covers and put a foot to the deck. Then he saw me, standing wide-legged to the roll of the vessel, slight though it was, with a sword in my hand and a pistol in my belt.

"You." He started to rise and I tilted the point of the blade at him. "Is it mutiny then?" he asked.

"Not mutiny, Captain, for I'm no sworn member

of your crew, nor legally taken on. The coast lies yonder, and I am taking my freedom."

"The savages will roast you," he warned.

"Me, at least, not you," I said. "Now, Captain, there's a matter between us, a matter of money taken from me, and a matter of payment for my work as a crew member. As well as damages."

"Damages! I'll damage you!" He lunged up, and I put my blade against his chest and pressed, just enough.

He cried out and fell back, a spot of blood on his shirt front. "The money taken from me, Captain. I'll take the rest in goods."

From his shirt he took my sack of money and threw it to me. Deftly I picked it from the air, hefting the weight. It felt right.

"My time is worth money, more than your ship, but I'll not take that. However," I said, "four hundred weight of trade goods as well as some powder and shot should do for damages."

"Four hundred weight!" He almost screamed it. "You're daft, man!"

"All right. Have it your own way, five hundred weight."

Bardle stared at me hard-eyed. "I should have dropped you over the side the first day out," he said. "I was a fool to waste time."

"No doubt," I replied cheerfully. "But you might have found trouble doing it, and you'd still have Tempany to settle with." I smiled at him. "You know, Bardle, you can never go back to England now."

"What's that? What d' you mean?"

"By now, inquiries will have traced me to your ship. You will be waited for when you return."

He did not like that. He tried to stare me down, to not believe what I had said, but he believed.

"Bah!" he sneered. "They'll not notice you! You're nothin' but a farmer from the fens!"

The cabin held little else that I wanted. A compass, which I took, another brace of pistols, which I also placed to one side. He watched me, his eyes bulging. "You're a bloody thief!" he shouted.

"Next time you think to knock some lad in the head, Bardle, remember this. And when I leave you, remember that Tempany is coming along behind you, and he knows your craft and you. He will be looking for you.

"The night after that on which you took me, I was to meet an Earl, Genester's cousin. He had plans in which I was concerned. Captain Tempany was also involved, as were others. Oh, you've done it this time, Bardle! You've fixed yourself nicely!"

Gathering what I needed in one hand and under that arm, I backed to the door. "Don't try coming out, Bardle, and don't try to follow me."

"You think Tempany will find you?" Bardle sneered. "No man knows this coast, not even Gosnold or Newport! Once you leave this vessel you'll not be seen again."

"Hadn't you guessed? I don't intend to be seen, not for a long time, Bardle. Not until after you've been drawn and quartered and hung in chains. You've been the death of many a poor lad. Now you can die for me."

At the steps I paused again. "I plan to trade with the savages, Bardle. I shall live here, gather a cargo of furs. And I shall return in a few years, a rich man.

"When I return to England, I shall go back and

74

see what remains of your body. By then they will probably have thrown your bones into potter's field."

"You're a coldblooded one, Sackett," he stared at me, his eyes sullen, "but the savages will deal with you."

I drew the door shut behind me and went up the ladder. All was quiet. Yet when I drew near the bulwark Sakim stepped out quickly. "Sackett, we'd better be ashore. I think something is stirring down below."

"Aye. Into the boat with you." I was rigging a sling for my additional goods as I spoke. All was dark and still, and there were no stars in the sky. From what talk I'd picked up, it was said this was a coast where terrible storms often struck.

Sakim went down a rope to the boat and stood by to cast off. Rufisco followed.

I had a leg over the railing when they came, and they came with a rush. They had found some opening forward of which I knew nothing, and they had gathered in the darkness there. They were close before I saw them and they came suddenly.

At the same moment, Nick Bardle burst from his cabin door, pistol in hand. Where he had the extra gun I did not know, but I shot at the mob rushing me, then threw my other leg over and slid down the rope.

In an instant, Bardle was there, pistol up, he took careful aim, but I hit the boat and Sakim cast off. Rufisco had stepped to the oars and he gave a terrific pull, backing instead of going forward. And the move saved my life.

The pistol bellowed, and the slug hit the bulwark near me with a thud.

Rufisco was shaking out some canvas, and the wind caught at it. We moved forward swiftly, but I held my fire, watching Bardle. He was no longer attempting to charge his pistol, just staring at me.

Once more only, I turned to look at the *Jolly Jack*. Her bow was swinging slowly toward the sea, for Bardle had no wish to be caught adrift on a lee shore. I looked, and then I turned my eyes away from the ship, away from the sea, away from England and home. Before me lay a continent, a vast sweep of land inhabited by savage men of whom I knew nothing. Nor had I any knowledge of how or when I might escape from this land, nor what awaited us upon landing.

I crawled aft, edging my way, for we were fearfully overloaded with goods. I took the tiller and sank down into place.

Off upon my left I could hear the rustle of surf upon the sand. It was a quiet night.

Sakim looked back from a place in the bow. "What do we do now?" he said.

A moment I hesitated, and then replied, "We find a haven before daylight, some place of concealment where we may hide ourselves and the gig. Then we will look about and see what manner of land we have come to."

It had been in my mind to trade for furs, to return to England a rich man. But now England seemed far, far away, and the land before me, vast, mysterious and unknown. This land was my destiny . . .

If I was to establish a family, it would be here in this land. And if they were to prosper here, it would have to be in such a way as the land demanded. I had no doubt those distant sons and grandsons would respond, that we Sacketts would establish a place for ourselves *here*, in this land, this America.

Chapter 8

The shore line was faintly visible, a vague white line off to our far right. Yet it was not in my thoughts to go immediately ashore, nor to beach the gig in some place near at hand simply to be soon ashore.

Some inlet, cove or small bay was what we needed, or some small, offshore island where we could conceal ourselves and the gig until we could decide what to do.

The phosphorescent water rolled back from the bow, the rigging of our small sail creaked pleasantly, and we sat still, not talking, filled with wonder at what we had done and were doing. On our right was the strange land, discovered more than one hundred years back, yet even now unknown. My mind was filled with awe as I remembered Tallis speaking of a great river found by Hernando de Soto, a mysterious river from out of nowhere that rushed away again into a vague somewhere . . .

"I am somewhat afraid," I spoke quietly, into the blackness. "It is a strange land into which we go."

"It is good to say that you are afraid," Sakim said. "It is not good to be too bold. A little fear makes a man think. It is better to be a little afraid, and yet do what has to be done."

"I think we must be bold with these savages," I said, "bold, yet respectful. They know us not. We must let them know we are not afraid, and that in our trade we wish only to be fair."

"My people traded across the world in ancient times," Sakim said. "Our ships went to India, China, and the Spice Islands. Even voyages around the world are talked of, and long before Magellan.

"It is written that when he found the Straits that were named for him he had a chart . . . Who made the chart? Who had been there before him? An Arab? A Chinese? Who? I think many civilizations have been born and have died before history was written."

"You would take the glory from Columbus?" Rufisco protested.

"Who knows how old is man?" Sakim said.

"There are tombs in Ireland," I commented, "from a thousand years before the pyramids were built."

The wind was freshening, and even our small sail was catching a pocketful, and the gig was moving along the shore, but well out from it. Suddenly the line of surf vanished and we found ourselves before an opening. Easing the tiller over, I took us into the bay. Whether it was large or small, I could not say.

Talk was well enough, I thought, but now what we needed was shelter. What little I knew of this coast was bad—terrible storms were known here, and tremendous seas.

When it came to that, I knew not if this were indeed the coast I believed it to be. Our charts were crude, and few had sailed the full length of the coast.

At Boston, where we frequently sailed from the

fens, I'd learned enough to know the Atlantic had been an obstacle, but never an insurmountable barrier. To cross it from Ireland was no great thing, and many an Irish, English or Breton seaman was amused by the talk of the Columbus "discovery." To them it was scarcely that, for they had been catching fish off the Grand Banks for nearly a hundred years.

There was a faint light in the sky now, and we could see clearly the gray line of coast with a white line of surf along the sand.

We were in some kind of a bay or sound, with open water to the south, and to the west a shore lined with trees. We edged that way, for it was no part of my plan to have daylight find us exposed to all eyes upon the open water.

We saw no sign of life along the shore, no plume of smoke. Yet there must be natives here, in such a place as this.

Rufisco called softly. "Look! There is an opening!"

I put the tiller over, and under a good head of wind we ran in toward the shore. There was a cove before us, with a half moon of beach, but nearer there was a smaller opening that seemed to be a creek mouth. As Sakim took in our sail, we ran up this creek until we saw a great dead tree that had fallen half in the water, half out. Sculling with an oar we worked close to it and tied up.

A bird sang and the water rustled. Overhead a white gull winged slowly past, dropping a curious glance our way.

Standing up, I belted on my blade, thrust pistols into my waistband and took up the fowling piece.

"No noise!" I warned. "Let us be very quiet. We are alone here, and we must know something of where we are."

We waded ashore, looking carefully around us. Some of the trees were pine, with here and there a gnarled and ancient oak, much brush of kind I did not know, and driftwood everywhere.

Our position seemed good. A small but deep creek flowed down through the sandhills on the opposite side of the cove which we had seen. There was perhaps an acre of ground scattered with driftwood and coarse grass that sloped down to the creek. It was ringed with trees, sheltered from all view.

"No fire," I said. "Break out some of the biscuit. We will eat that."

Rufisco went back to the boat to get the biscuit and Sakim went further inland. Soon he was back. "There is a spring whose water is not bad." He had some slender sticks in his hand. "I shall make a bow," he said, "and arrows."

After we had eaten lightly, careful of the food we had brought ashore, I left Sakim at making his bow and went inland, moving quietly, working my way to what seemed the highest of the sandhills.

When I reached it there was a good view on all sides. Toward the sea and to the south was a broad sound, protected from the sea by barrier islands of sand. There was no sign of a sail, yet I could not believe we had gotten away so easily, nor that Nick Bardle would rest content.

Further along the shore I found where a fire had been built, but the ends of charred wood that remained were old. There were many shells there where Indians, or whoever the fire-builders had been, had eaten shellfish.

Many grassy meadows lay back from the shore, a fair land indeed, and promising well for future farmers, if such there came to be. Nowhere did I see any signs of recent men—only the remains of fires and a few sticks cut by some crude implement.

I saw many ducks and geese, and several times brown and somewhat speckled birds flew up, very large birds, many of them as big as geese. These must be the turkeys of which Gosnold had told.

After a while, I came down to the bank of the stream on which we had camped, but far above our camp site. It was enough to tell me that this river offered no access to the higher country. That must be found elsewhere.

On high ground again I sat down just to look and to study.

We must find a river, sail up the river and inland for a short distance, then establish a base. Part of our goods we would bury, and carefully conceal the place of hiding. If attacked or robbed we must not lose all. Then I must approach some strong chieftain and establish an alliance with him, and choose a site on the river for a town.

A river-crossing not too far from the sea, a place where Indians were used to come, yet reachable by ocean vessels. For it was in my mind to establish a trading post which would grow into a city. Rome had begun at a river crossing, and London, too.

Now we were in new land, a free land, a land to be shaped as we wished, and I hoped then that those who came after me would want, as I wanted, a safe land for people, for homes, for freedom.

All this was good, this open land. I thought of the crowded streets of London, of the poor I had seen there, and of many of the men with whom I'd worked in the quarries, each hungry for his own bit of land. Why not here?

Not all the land for a few great lords, but a piece

of land for each man, land to grow crops, to keep bees and a cow.

Suddenly there was movement. Below me, moving in single file, four savages moved stealthily. Four armed with bows, moving toward the point on which we had camped!

Four of them, three of us, but we were scattered, and neither Sakim nor Rufisco knew of their coming.

Four . . . and they were painted for war. I had heard of that.

My position was a good one, for I stood close to the trunk of a huge oak, thicker than two of me; and beside me were others, almost as large. There were fallen timbers about; it was not an easy place to approach.

What to do? I hesitated to shoot a man who had not seen me, yet if I didn't they would stalk and kill me if they could.

And if they were allowed to go on they would find my friends and perhaps kill them, too.

Something brushed leaves behind me, and I turned swiftly. An Indian stood there, but he lifted his hand, palm out. "No enemy you," he said, and he pointed at the four warriors in the trail below "There enemy!"

A half dozen Indians came up through the trees, and scarcely glancing at me, sifted through the brush and trees along the hillside.

"I am Barnabas," I said. "I come to trade and to learn."

"I am Potaka. I speak white man many time. I friend."

"I have two friends." I held up two fingers. "There. . . ." I pointed. "No hurt."

He was gone, and I waited. For several minutes I

waited, heard a piercing yell, then a running and a movement in the brush.

Suddenly, one of the Indians I had seen in the trail below came running toward me. There was a long scratch on his arm and he carried a bloody knife. He rushed through the brush and burst into the clearing where I stood.

For a moment he stopped, as if transfixed, but I stared back at him and made no move. He looked, grunted something, then was gone. Obviously, I had astonished him.

Potaka came back, on the run. "He come?"

"That way," I pointed. "He came, and he fled. Very quick."

Potaka hesitated, then sheathed his knife. "It is enough. We kill two."

"You speak very good English."

He smiled broadly. "Me friend Englishman. No friend Espanish. Sometime Espanish fight us. Sometime English fight Espanish. One time Englishman, Potaka fight Espanish together. You like?"

"Your village is near?"

"Far . . . two sleeps." He pointed inland. "You come?"

"Later."

Potaka looked about. "You are only three?"

"Our ship comes back soon," I said, casually. "We were left to find friendly Indians who wish to trade. We wish to trade knives, needles, and cloth for furs."

"Come to my village. Welcome. No parlay to them. They kill."

He was a man of medium height, strong, no darker than many a Portuguese, and quick in his movements. His expression was friendly, and there was much about him I liked.

"We fight Espanish many time," he said. "English-man live among us . . . long time."

"Is he with you now?"

"No more. He live four, five year, then he say he see behind mountains. Maybe seven moons pass. Maybe dead now."

From my belt I took a knife. It was keen of blade, and as long as my forearm. I extended it to him, haft first. "For you, my friend," I said, and gave it to him.

He knelt suddenly, tracing with his finger in the dust. He pointed to the river nearby. Then with his finger he showed the river, a trail leading from it. "Village here," he said. "You come."

He picked up his spear. "You come," he repeated, and then he was gone.

I waited, listening. There was no sound for a long time, and so I went down through the trees toward our camp, and after a long walk, arrived there.

Rufisco greeted me. Sakim emerged from the willows. "There was fighting?" Rufisco asked.

"Among the Indians," I said, "and I may have made a friend."

"I do not trust them," Rufisco muttered. "They are savages."

"What is a savage?" I asked, shrugging. "It is another way of life. We will be cautious, my friends, we will be bold and we will be honest. If that does not work, we will fight—when the time comes.

"There are many of them and only three of us. I think it would be well to remember this. My friend is Potaka. He says the others are to be avoided."

"What do they say of Potaka?" Rufisco asked.

I shrugged. "Probably the same thing, but until we know, we will be careful. And the Eno has invited us to his village."

"You are going?"

"We came to trade. I gave him a gift, a trade knife. Sometimes a blade can open a door."

When darkness came and our smoke would not be visible, we built a fire in a hollow and baked some fish Sakim had caught. "We will move," I said. "when we have eaten. We will find a new camp."

The night was a time of stillness. Frogs croaked, and several times we heard great roarings in the distance. "Lions?" Rufisco asked.

"Alligators," Sakim said. "I have heard them on the Nile. We must be careful, my friend. Do not step upon or over a log until you are sure it is a log, and watch the tail. They will try to break your legs or knock you into the water with their tails."

"It is very dark," Rufisco said. "Can we not rest before we move?"

I was myself tired. "Sakim? You will take the first watch? One hour only, then awaken Rufisco. One hour, and then awaken me. I will watch for an hour and then we will go. It will be a little rest for each."

It seemed no time until I was awakened, and when Rufisco lay asleep I sat and listened into the night. Behind me, stretching no man knew how far, a strange land. To right and left a lonely coast where likely lay only the wrecks of ships carried here by storms or currents in the sea.

Soon we would move . . . toward what? Would I die here and leave only my bones for legacy? Or would some strange destiny begin here, in this place, so the name of Sackett became one with this new, strange land?

It was clouding over, and there was a hint of

dampness on the wind. Rain? It would help us. It would conceal our movements, erase our tracks.

I touched each upon each shoulder. "Sakim! Rufisco! It is time."

Chapter 9

The rain came with a rush of heavy drops, a scattering like thrown gravel. Then the massed downpour of the storm descended, pushing inward from the sea, an invader like us.

Against the wind and rain we went upstream, up this nameless river, past timbered shores and swamplike meadows. The wind held, and our sail moved us along, the driving rain offering some concealment.

Huddling in our cloaks we watched the dim shores slip past, and then the wind slackened, our sail gave us scarcely any movement against the current, and we unshipped oars and pointed on an angle for the left bank.

"How far would you say we've come?" I asked.

Sakim shrugged. "The current is strong. I doubt more than ten, twelve of your English miles."

Before us we saw a long rocky island, lying several lengths away from our gig. We steered closer, and finding an opening, steered in.

Two of us scrambled ashore and hauled the boat up onto the sand. "Only what we need," I said. "Let's be ready to shove off if trouble comes."

Under an overhang we built a small fire of drift-wood and warmed our chilled hands.

"We will cache a part of what we have," I suggested, "and then we will trade with Potaka's people. We will be fair."

"Is it fair," Rufisco asked, "to trade beads worth a few pennies for a fox skin worth as many guineas?"

"Of course. Value is a matter of scarcity and need. The beads we have cost little in England because we have many, but here those beads are rare. Furs are cheap to them for the same reasons. We want their furs, they want our beads. So we strike a bargain.

"They cannot sell a fox skin here for what it is worth in England because they are not in England. We will trade carefully, gather many furs. and then we will go back to the sea and wait for a ship, for Gosnold, Newport, Weymouth or any who come."

"Including Nick Bardle?"

"Him we will try to avoid."

None of us could know for sure what lay before us. But each of us hoped to become rich. Sakim was a man long away from his home. Rufisco wished to go back in a blaze of glory, with fine clothes, excellent weapons, and a name of importance.

There was a restlessness in me, an urge to be doing, and I knew it was not only myself who thought or felt in such a way. It was an urge to see, to know, to discover. A part of my age,   my time, it was in the blood of us all, I suspected, even of Rufisco, despite his claims to the contrary.

I added a chunk of driftwood to the fire. The ashes at the edge of the fire were dry, white, powdery. I sifted them through my fingers.

Night settled about us like a falling shroud. Night, and the rain, a soft, steady rain now. Fortunately there was driftwood aplenty and I kept the fire small but warm.

Sakim and Rufisco had fallen asleep. After a while I got up, looking carefully around in the dim light. This place was a good one, the overhangs offered shelter from wind and rain. After midnight the rain let up and I walked out on the sand and looked up at the rock under which we were sheltered. The forest came right up to the jumble of rocks, and there were great, gray giants of trees lying dead upon the rocks, blown down in some terrible storm, no doubt.

I lay down and slept, awakening as I wished before it was light. All was still. There was no rain, but the clouds hung low. Taking up my sword and my own dagger which I had retrieved from the bales of goods, I sought a way to climb the rocks. At first I could find none, then I found a crack, an opening scarce wide enough for my body. Worming my way to the top I managed by a precarious foothold to climb a steep slanted rock up into the forest—a dark tangle of fallen trees, tangled brush, moss, and low-growing branches. There was no evidence that any man had ever come this way.

For a long time I sat there on a log, studying the layout. It was such a tangle that it invited no exploration. Indians in search of game could find it in easier places than this.

After a while I returned to the fire. The others were still asleep, so I added fuel to the glowing embers and continued to explore. High at the opposite corner of the beach from where I had first found my way up, I saw a dark hole under some fallen boulders. Stooping, I went inside. It was not a natural cave, just a space left under some slabs of rock. Yet it went deeply back, and after a few feet inside I could straighten up. Light came from small openings between boulders.

Clambering up on one side, I found a good shelf, slanting back about fifteen feet.

Here was what I had sought. A storage place for our surplus goods!

When I returned to the fire, Rufisco was up. Not only up, but he had caught three good-sized fish which he was broiling over the coals.

Sakim joined us at the fire, extending his hands to the flames. I told them what I had discovered, and when we had eaten our fish and a bit of biscuit, we moved our cargo ashore, holding out enough for an eighty-pound pack for each. Then we cached the remainder on the rock shelf in the cave.

When we had finished, Rufisco spoke to me.

"We have come with you, Barnabas," he said, "because we like you, and because anything was better than to live and die on Bardle's ship. But what is it you plan?"

"Before Bardle waylaid me, I was to have come here with a ship captained by Brian Tempany," I replied. "He was to sail a few days after the *Jolly Jack*. His ship is the *Tiger*. She was a slower sailer than the *Jack*, and should be along the coast within the next few weeks. She will be trading with the Indians, and exploring. Her route was the same.

"What I hope to do is make trade with the Eno Indians, take our furs and be back on the coast to meet the *Tiger*, should it come near. It is a chancy thing, as you can see, but if the *Tiger* does not come there will be others."

"And then?"

"For a time I want to stay. If all goes well, I shall trade my share of the furs for more goods and remain here. After a year I will sail again to England."

Rufisco's smile was ironic. "If you live."

"Of course. Here or in England, all plans await the decision of the Master."

The Lord had my trust, yet of others I was not so sure. The Indians were an uncertainty, and so was Nick Bardle. He was a hard, vengeful man. Would he leave matters as they stood?

"This Potaka," Rufisco asked, "you trust him?"

"He seemed friendly, yet we will proceed with caution," I replied.

Rufisco hoisted our sail, once we had rowed clear of our hide-out, and catching a good wind we started upstream and made good time.

I kept a sharp lookout along the banks to see what manner of trees there might be, for one in particular I sought.

Amazing was the variety. There was much willow and alder. I saw beech, tulip, poplar, several kinds of pine, birch, hemlock, chestnut, and the white limbs of buckeye. Further along I spotted here and there a sycamore, an ash, an elm. It was in my mind to make longbows and arrows for silent hunting as well as to conserve our supply of gunpowder.

Several times we saw smoke, and once we passed a considerable village with huts that seemed, at the distance, to be made of bark. There was the smoke of a half-dozen fires there, and numerous canoes drawn up on the banks. Dogs ran down and barked angrily, but we were some distance off and we saw no Indians until we had rounded the bend, when at the last moment I looked back and saw several, whether men or women I could not tell, emerge from their huts.

"Did they see us?" Rufisco wondered.

"It is possible," I said, "but they came late."

Even as I spoke I was looking ahead. The shore of the river curved in and the river narrowed. It was a bad place, bringing us dangerously close to the banks.

Sakim spoke suddenly. "Barnabas! Look!"

He pointed. Several Indians appeared momentarily in the willows, running abreast of us. Then another, farther ahead, moving toward the narrow passage where we would be closest in.

Glancing toward the passage, I saw no Indians, just some large dead trees projecting into the water and making the narrow gap even more dangerous. The wind was only fairly good. "Get out the oars," I told Rufisco, "we're going to need them."

I took my fowling piece from the thwart and looked to the priming, then replaced it. The last thing we wanted was a fight.

I watched the stream, the shore, and held the tiller steady. No Indians appeared.

Nearer . . . nearer. Sakim put his hand down to his musket.

No Indians. The sandy shores were empty. There seemed no movement in the trees and brush beyond. I glanced upstream. If we could just get through the gap . . .

Suddenly, Rufisco grunted. Turning I saw three Indians emerge from the brush, running hard. Behind them a fourth . . . a fifth.

The first one came quickly to a halt, lifted his bow and let fly an arrow. The distance was right but he had been too eager, and the arrow fell astern.

A second arrow hit my pack, just ahead of me. A third flew over. Rufisco lifted his musket and fired.

The heavy *boom* of the musket was like thunder.

An Indian cried out and fell. As Rufisco re-loaded, I saw the Indian trying to rise, a great slash across his thigh. He fell, blood covering his leg, and the others stood still as if frozen, staring and frightened.

Rufisco put down his musket and took up the oars, dipping them deep to help the sail. Soon we were out of the Indians' range. Rufisco's face was pale, his eyes large as he stared at me. "Why do they wish to kill us, Barnabas?" he asked.

"We are strangers. We are not of their tribe, and they fear us. And we have goods . . . what we have is a great treasure to them. It is the way of the world, Rufisco."

"But we come for trade!"

"Aye, and so did some of the ships taken at sea by privateers or pirates. We will trade with whomever we can, but we will take nothing by capture unless we are first attacked."

"They will have no such feelings."

"I do not know. Perhaps, perhaps not."

The gig was moving smoothly upstream now. At a fork, we turned right, gliding between low banks with scattered clumps of trees and some marsh. We saw no Indians, but twice we saw deer, and several flocks of wild turkeys.

Suddenly I remembered something. The fine gray ash at the edge of our campfire.

Potash . . .

There was a need for potash in England, and a fine market for it. One need not think only of furs, and the potash could be obtained by burning driftwood.

A prosaic cargo, certainly, but a needful one.

Suddenly, Sakim cried out, and I looked up from my daydreaming.

We had rounded a bend, and coming toward us,

so close there could be no escape, a dozen canoes . . .
perhaps forty men . . . and all were armed.

"Stand fast!" I said sharply. "Hold your fire!"

Chapter 10

My first realization, after an immediate stab of fear,
was that the Indians wore no paint. There were stories
enough in England about Indians painting for war.

"Put your weapons out of sight," I said, "below
the gunwhales. I think they are peaceful."

The canoes slowed their pace, gliding down to
us, and then a hand lifted, palm outward, and I
recognized Potaka.

"It is my friend," I explained.

Rufisco snorted. "No Indian is your friend," he
said. "Keep your gun handy."

I lifted my hand in a sign of peace, and Potaka
glided close. If he saw the guns he made no sign of
it, nor showed it by gesture or expression. "You
come to village?"

"We come," I said.

"Good!"

He shouted to the others and they turned their
canoes with a deft, easy maneuver and ranged alongside us, before and aft.

Sunlight sparkled on the river as the clouds scattered before a warm south wind. Beside us, the grace-
ful birch-bark canoes glided easily through the water, the copper arms of the Indians moving in unison.

It was no small journey we had undertaken. Now they led the way, and we kept pace, certain only that we had small choice. Their attitude was friendly, but how could we know how genuine it was?

At night we camped ashore, and their hunters brought in meat in plenty. Good venison it was, such as a man might not have in England without poaching on the estate of some great lord.

The Indians were of short stature, and only a few of them were muscular except with the long, lean muscles that indicate the runner. At wrestling I had no doubt I could best any one of them, perhaps any two.

They talked much among themselves, and laughed a lot.

When we reached their village we found it was extensive, many huts of wattle and daub construction, surrounding an open field.

All were busy, and they seemed to have a considerable store of grain. Potaka told me they had three harvests each year and traded with less industrious tribes nearby. There was much dressing of skins, parching of acorns, and gathering of herbs from the forest.

Several times Potaka showed me men who had been injured in battle, occasionally with tribes of Indians, but usually with the "Espanish," whose northward movement they had attempted to stop.

They were avid for trade, but we were cautious, telling them they must await the coming of our ship for extensive trade, that we had but little. We began cautiously enough, displaying only a few articles. I was surprised, for they were an industrious folk and wanted needles, knives and axes more than beads and fripperies.

On the first day we traded but little, and when the feasting began we contributed from our small store. Potaka made a great speech, which he translated in part as an account of his warfare on the side of the English against the Spanish, a speech he had no doubt made before, but which his fellows cheered lustily.

We talked much of the land about us, and Potaka traced routes on the ground, using his finger or a twig to trace in the dirt.

One he indicated. "Warriors' Path," he said. He pointed at the western horizon, then drew a wavy line and with gestures indicated that he described a mountain ridge. At one point he pointed out a low place in the mountains, a wide gap. "Here Warriors' Path," he said.

"And beyond?"

"Much good hunt, but much fight also. Many tribes come there, none stay. Is good place, but dangerous place!"

"Someday," I said to Potaka, "I want to travel that road."

He looked at me thoughtfully. "It is long trail, many dangers."

"There is game beyond the mountains?"

He described the deer, fox, bear, lion, buffalo.

For two days more we traded, bringing out a few things each time, trading with care. Our stack of furs grew, and even Rufisco was feeling good. On the fourth day our English goods were gone, and we packed our furs into a canoe.

"We go now, for more goods," I said. "We will come again to trade."

"Killers there," Potaka pointed downstream. "You go by night."

The whole village was down at the shore to wave good-bye, and when our canoe rounded a bend and they were lost to sight, Rufisco grunted, then said, "You were right. But who knows how it will be next time?"

"We have made a profit," I said quietly. "We have rich furs, but it is a beginning only."

"Aye," Rufisco agreed, "the furs are good. Such furs I have not seen except Russian. But you do not have them in a market, my friend. There is a long river before us, and at the end of the river a large ocean and maybe Nick Bardle!"

"You think he is waiting for us?"

"Waiting and trading, and such men make no friends for the white man. He'll be waiting, searching. He will go first to the shore. He will talk to the Indians, seek out those who have seen us or found some sign of our going, then he will study the rivers . . . and how many can there be? Three? Four, perhaps? Not so many that he cannot watch.

"If we do not come soon, he will know we are dead, if we do come he will make sure we are dead. The problem is not so difficult, eh?

"You say, 'It is a big country, how can he find us?' But I say it is easy to find us. It is not a big country when there are white men in a boat. In all this country there can be but one boat with white men, perhaps but one boat with a sail. So he will find us."

"You are a pessimist," I grumbled, yet some of my complacency was gone. There was truth in what he said.

"A pessimist," Rufisco agreed, "but no fool."

"We will enter our hiding place at night," I said. "Of that we must be sure. We will cache our furs there, get more trade goods, and be off once more."

"But not to Potaka's people," Sakim suggested. "We have the best of their furs."

That was another thing I had not considered. Who next? And where? I must prepare and plan.

We eased downstream, making good time with the current, and slipped from the narrow waters of the Eno stream into the main current of the larger river up which we had come. We saw no one.

Later in the day, under the drooping branches of a tree on the shore of a small island, we fed ourselves. Ashore, we gathered some grapes, drank from a small spring, and waited out the remainder of the day. Only when it was full dark did we slip away from our moorings, and slide down stream with the current. Midnight was long past when we saw the loom of our rocks.

All was quiet and still. For a moment after we glided into the inner channel we sat very still, listening. There was the lap of water against our hull. . . nothing more.

At daybreak we were awake and moved our furs ashore, re-stocking the gig with trade goods, taking the same amount as before. Yet we did not at once move out.

We lay about resting, mending clothes, preparing for what lay ahead. And I busied my hands with making a bow and arrows.

For three days we rested, doing the small chores, the mending and fixing that needed being done, and each day, several times each day, one of us climbed on top and climbed a tree. We saw no sign of the *Jolly Jack*, nor of any other ship on the sound. On the fourth day I killed a fair-sized buck with my bow. We butchered it, and began drying the meat. On the fifth day I killed again, another buck, smaller and younger.

We sorted and re-packed our skins. They were fox, mink, otter, beaver and muskrat.

On the fifth night, well after dark, we eased from our hide-out and started upstream once more. This time we went not so far, turning left up the river we had passed en route to Potaka's people. We traveled up this river some distance and, seeing the smoke of a village in the light of the moon, we turned toward the shore. When we were quite close in we stopped, dropped our anchor and lay offshore in such wise that if the natives appeared warlike we could up our anchor and sail and go quickly hence.

Then, while Sakim and I slept, Rufisco watched. And when dawn was close, he slept and remained on watch. Then all of us saw the village awaken, saw them see us and heard their alarmed cries. Soon a number of warriors were coming toward the shore. I had made ready a fishing line and now I threw it into the water and sat placidly, fishing.

They came to the water's edge and shouted at us, and I lifted a hand, then motioned to the fishing line. After a moment the nibble I had became a bite, and I swiftly pulled in a good-sized fish.

I held up the big fish, then rubbed my stomach, and several Indians chuckled. I made signs to ask if I might come ashore.

They motioned for me to come, so guiding the gig in close, after heaving up the anchor, I let it drift close, keeping an eye that she did not ground. I dropped the anchor again, bade Sakim and Rufisco cover me, and went ashore.

My eyes went quickly over them. Only a few were armed, those who happened to be when our boat was seen. But all wore knives, most of them chipped obsidian. I saw but one steel knife among them, obviously old, and quite rusted.

Soon my companions were also ashore. This village was not so prosperous as Potaka's, yet well situated, and the Indians were friendly. We ate with them, talked of trails with sign language, and we traded. We saw numerous scalps, some of them quite fresh, and learned they had recently returned from a war party far to the north. One of the Indians, named Nikonha, had a few words of English. With words, sign language and a twig in the sand, we managed to converse. He was quick to perceive, and when he asked how we had come, I drew him a quick sketch of the ship.

He nodded quickly, then pointed eastward toward the shore.

He had seen the pinnace, he assured me, two suns past at a river-mouth. The pinnace was in the river, concealed in a bight near the south shore.

"Sakim," I spoke quietly, not to warn the Indians that anything was amiss, "this one has seen the *Jack*."

"Laying for us," Rufisco said.

We continued to trade.

I had put forward a handsome hunting knife when suddenly a big hand shot out and grasped it.

I looked up from where I sat into the eyes of a squatting Indian. He was a big fellow, very muscular, with a scar on his cheekbone. There was no friendliness in his eyes. "No trade," he said. "You give."

"Trade," I replied quietly, staring right back at him.

He grunted. "No trade," he repeated, and then he said, "I take."

The other Indians stood about, watching.

"Trade," I replied.

He started to sheath the knife but my hand grasped his wrist. "Trade," I said quietly, and my grip tightened.

He tried to lift his hand but could not. I saw the surprise, almost shock in his eyes. He tugged but his hand, grasping the knife, could not budge.

Angry blood flushed his face, but he could not move his hand. He tried to exert the strength of his thighs to lift it, but I held tight, not moving, undisturbed.

"Trade?" I asked quietly.

"Trade," he said sullenly.

Chapter 11

Through the dark waters the gig glided smoothly. Sakim was in the bow.

Our sail was furled as we wished to offer no silhouette to be seen from the shore. We were loaded to the gunwhales with furs, excellent furs, though perhaps not of the quality of our first load.

None of us had any illusions about what would happen if Bardle discovered our whereabouts, so we approached our base in the rocks with great caution.

It had began to rain, a soft, drizzling rain. We huddled in our boat, edging in toward shore. The rocks loomed before us, barely visible, like the shore. We touched the water with our oars.

Working in closer, ghostlike, we ran our gig up into the sand. Sakim got out to haul it firmer aground.

Fowling piece in hand, I stepped down to the sand.

It was very quiet, only the soft rain falling, and the whisper of the rain upon the water. "Stay with the boat," I whispered, and then walked forward alone in the darkness.

The space under the over-hang was empty, yet I was not reassured. Something about the place was wrong, very wrong. Retreating to the boat, I whispered, "Ease her back on the water, Sakim, and stand by to shove off."

"There is something?"

"Nothing. . . only I have a feeling."

"I, too."

Could they have found the cave where lay our furs? Were they waiting there? It was possible they could find the cave but not the furs.

"I want to sleep," Rufisco said, irritably. "And I am hungry."

"Better to wait for food," I said, "than try to digest cold steel."

Moving back along the shore, I circled warily toward the cave. Suddenly I heard uncalled-for sounds. I stood stock-still and listened.

The crack of a breaking stick, then another. The sound of flint against stone. Somebody was building a fire. I turned around.

Rufisco! He had come ashore and already had a small blaze going.

I swore bitterly, under my breath, and had taken a step toward him when suddenly the night exploded with a rush of human bodies.

They charged the fire.

The attackers had eyes only for the fire, perhaps could see only it.

Suddenly, Nick Bardle's voice roared through the

falling rain: "Damn you all to Hell! There's only one! Who gave the word? Where are the others?"

Turning, I crept toward the shore, hoping, praying, that Sakim would be near and waiting in the boat. I eased through the dark water, over my ankles, my knees . . . A hand from utter darkness caught me. It was Sakim.

Handing him my fowling piece and sword, I swung silently and thankfully aboard.

Rufisco was dead or a prisoner. There was nothing we could do to help him at the moment. We could help him best by retaining our freedom, our mobility.

Sakim wasted no time. He dipped the oars into the water very gently and sculled the boat deeper into the darkness.

Ashore there were angry arguments and shouts. Then I clearly heard Bardle. "Where are they? Damn you! Tell me or I'll slit your gullet!"

"I am alone," Rufisco's voice carried well, as no doubt he intended. "The others have gone upstream after furs. I was left to hunt for meat. . . ."

Then their voices were lost.

How long until dawn? Dared we try to slip around the rock into the river? We might be visible a few minutes only, but if they saw us. . .

How had they found us? By boat? Or overland, on foot through the woods?

We eased the boat along by pushing with our hands upon the rock wall. Now the voices were less plain.

We rounded a corner of the rock. The opening was before us, seeming much too light now for our wishes, but Sakim sat to the oars, and taking breath, he dipped deep and shot the boat forward as best he might, laden as she was. She moved well and he dipped his oars again. Suddenly from the shoreside there came a great shout and somebody fired, yet I had slight fear now of a hit, for we were some distance off and moving faster. Another dip of the oars and we caught the first suggestion of the river's current, then more, and we were swept through the passage.

It was no part of my plan to desert Rufisco. First we must find a place to cache our furs. Then, with the gig lightened, we might move with more freedom.

When dawn was brighter, we lifted our sail and started across river to the far side. There was little time, but we made to the shelter of an unpromising island and pointed toward shore. It was low, offering less visible shelter, yet there were some trees and shrubs about and clumps of willows.

"They would not think to look there," Sakim said. as if reading my mind. "We can find a place."

We sailed into shore, dropped our canvas and tied up to a huge old drift log with more branches than a porcupine, and waded ashore, keeping low.

Sakim betook himself to one end of the island, I to the other. Then a low call from him and I turned back.

He was waiting for me, and led me into the willows where I stopped, astonished indeed.

There lay, among the willows, the bow and a portion of the hull of a goodly vessel, almost buried in sand. How many years she had lain there, no man could say, but the stout oak timbers were still strong, and her sides formed a roof. Entering the shelter thus formed, we found the Captain's quarters intact, although lying sideways and half-filled with sand. Yet here was a shelter from the weather for our furs, though hopefully for a few days only.

We carried the bales inside, covering them with broken willow branches and reeds.

Returning to the gig, we shoved off, raised our sail and crossed back to a safe distance from home shore.

Our gig anchored, we crept back overland to the rocks, but they were deserted. All was still as death in the cloudy light, the sand churned by charging feet, a spot or two of blood.

"They will have returned to their vessel," I said. "We must follow."

"You will try to get him back?"

"He is one of us. We will have him back, if he lives."

"He is but bait for the trap," Sakim replied. "It is you they want."

"Nevertheless, he was one of us. You are with me?"

"Where you go, I follow."

If there was a sun that day it remained unseen, for there were lowering clouds and raindrops dripping from leaves in branches. We found the narrow game trail they had taken, but we turned aside from it and searched out another, almost parallel.

The fowling piece I left on the gig, but took my sword, dagger, bow and arrows. Sakim recharged a brace of the pistols and took them along, tucked in his sash. He also carried his scimitar and a spear.

It was wet under the trees. The path was slippery, but we moved in silence, pausing from time to time to listen for what we might hear, and we heard nothing. We covered what must have been a mile, then found ourselves climbing, ever so slightly. At the end of the second hour we reached the crest of a low hill that gave us a view of all that laid east and south of us, and there, not half a mile away, was the *Jolly Jack*.

For all my confident talk I knew not what to do to recover our companion, only that it must be done. And done by wit and wile rather than strength of arm and hand.

We worked our way down through brush and trees, avoiding the trail that might be guarded, until finally we came to the edge of a high woods not one hundred and fifty feet from the *Jolly Jack*. We were well hidden.

There could be but one reason for Bardle not killing Rufisco immediately. They hoped to have from him our hiding place. To save him suffering, we must somehow free him at once.

"What is there to do?" Sakim whispered, staring at the vessel.

A man with a cross-bow loitered near the ladder. On the shore nearby were several crude huts, hastily built of ship's canvas, driftwood poles and the like. A fire was blazing on the shore.

This was no place found by accident, but one known to Bardle or someone else aboard, for the bank was steep and the vessel lay in close, one line running from the bow to an oak tree, the other from the stern.

"They are close," I commented.

Sakim shrugged. "In my country we run our ships on the sand, then let the tide float them clear. It has always been so."

"Here there is a current," I said thoughtfully, studying the water on which they lay, as much as it could be seen. "Another river must come into the sound from somewhere west of them."

"There he is. They did not take him aboard," Sakim said suddenly. He pointed. "Two of those with him just came from that hut."

I could see them. If they would just leave Rufisco there, and if we could create a diversion. . .

They were a rough, ugly lot, and I had no desire to see them go to work on Rufisco. He was a good man, if surly and given to sarcasm and doubt—too good a man to be tortured by this lot of scoundrels, who were little better than pirates.

It worried me that they should have chosen to stop at this place, for it was my wish to establish good relations with the savages. With such a lot as the crew of the *Jolly Jack* it would be impossible, for they were a pack of greedy brutes.

"There is a thought, Sakim," I said, "a thought that has come to me."

He glanced at me. "It must be a good thought," Sakim suggested, "I think there is not much time, and they are very many."

Turning, I led the way back into the woods, circling wide around toward the shore. There was a thing I must know. My father had always told me the way to win was to attack. No matter how outnumbered, there was always a good way to attack.

It was a little time before we came to our objective. It was the tree to which the upstream line was made fast. "It is a strong current," I said.

Sakim squatted on his haunches, his teeth flashing through the darkness of his pointed beard. "A strong current," he agreed. "And if this line were cut——?"

Crouching close, I noticed there was no watch on the line. Nobody was closer than us to the ship itself, and the line was a good long one. It was made fast around the lower trunk of the tree, and heavily screened by brush.

"The big roots will help," I said, "but we must build up some shelter with mud."

"Mud?"

"We will not cut the line," I said, "because both of us will be needed to rescue Rufisco. We must be *there* when the line breaks, not here. We will start a fire, a very small fire, and leave it burning. It will be screened by roots and mud as well as the brush. When the line gives way, we will be ready and waiting."

Sakim considered, then nodded. "Allah be with us," he said. "It is a fearsome thing we do."

Carefully we prepared our small fire, and added fuel. It began to burn; flames touched the heavy line. Adding a little fuel, we turned and went swiftly back to our former place.

Now we must hope. If the fire did not die out, or if it was not discovered and killed, then the line must part. Caught by the current the stern would swing into the stream, turning counter-clockwise. All hands would immediately rush to save their ship, and then, if all went as we hoped. . .

We waited . . . and waited. Nothing happened.

The same two men stood at the door of the hut where Rufisco was likely imprisoned. Others were gathered about their cooking fires. I notched an arrow and looked at the man nearest me by the hut.

All was quiet. The vessel lay gently upon the waters, only straining a little at the lines. Had our fire gone out? Had someone discovered it?

Suddenly there was a sharp cracking sound as the line parted, and instantly the stern of the ship swung into the current. Somebody let go with a wild yell, and there were shouts and running from aboard the vessel. Men dashed toward the bow where a rope-ladder hung.

"Now," I said, and we went forward, not running,

but walking carefully, swiftly. A step, two steps. . .
The heavier guard turned and I let fly my arrow. It
was high, but lucky. It took the guard in the throat
and he fell, grasping the arrow's shaft with both
hands.

Around the shore there were wild yells, shouts, orders, recriminations.

The second guard had run out a small way, and
Sakim put an arm across his throat and a knife into
his ribs. I ducked into the hut.

Rufisco, barely visible in reflected firelight, was
struggling. I slipped my blade under his bonds and
the razor edge parted them. "Rub your legs," I said.
"We'll have to run."

"I can run," he replied grimly, and we ducked outside. I sheathed my sword and took up the bow again.

I notched an arrow and followed, backing up,
watching to cover our retreat.

My eyes were seeking Nick Bardle. An arrow for
him and I would consider myself well paid.

Just one arrow!

He was there, but shifting about among the running men, and there was no good target. "Another
time, Captain," I told myself. "Another time."

I turned and walked into the woods, and in a few
minutes had caught up with my friends.

We had been quick, but lucky too. I had no good
feeling about that luck of ours. It was too good. It
was building us for a smashing blow. . . I could feel
it in my bones.

Chapter 12

We found our way to our gig. Under the shelter of the shrubs and trees we slept, awakened, cooked a meal, then slept again.

Finally when my eyes opened the others still slept, and I lay awake, a lonely man, thinking back to England, the fens, and even more to a girl with a lamp in her hand. I'd no cause to be thinking of her, yet each man has some girl he thinks of, and my thoughts kept turning back to her.

We Sacketts had a feeling for home and family, and although I'd had no family but my father, the sense was strong within me. Now we had furs, one half of which were mine. It was a goodly sum, but insufficient. We must go along the coast and keep a sharp lookout for the *Tiger*, Tempany's ship. By now it might be near.

If we could exchange our furs for more trade goods, another venture might be even more profitable.

Rufisco awakened as I was broiling a piece of venison.

"I have not thanked you," he said.

"It is not important." I stirred the coals. "You would have done the same for me."

He sat up. "Perhaps. I have been wondering about that."

"Well," I said, "in my place you would have."

"Your place?"

"I was your leader. I was responsible. It makes a difference, you know."

He chuckled grimly. "I avoid leadership. I do not wish to decide such things, nor to be responsible."

With my knife I cut off a sliver of my meat, burning my fingers in the process. "When you and Sakim chose to come with me I accepted responsibility for your lives. I became no longer a free agent. Unless one is at heart a rascal, I think he becomes a little better in many ways by assuming leadership."

"You may have it." He reached for a chunk of the meat, impaled in on a stick and held it to the flames. "And now what, Oh Mighty Leader?"

"We go to sea. If she survived the crossing, the *Tiger* may now be alongshore. I saw her charts, and it was toward this place she intended to come."

"And then?"

"Exchange our furs and return to trading."

"For you . . . not for me."

"No?"

"I have a foreboding upon me. This land is not for me. I shall return to Naples, or even to Florence or to Ravenna. I shall bask in the sun on a terrace somewhere and watch the pretty girls go by. I shall drink wine and smell the smells. . . No, my friend, I want to live."

He gestured widely. "I have no taste for wilderness like this. I do not like swamps, lonely beaches and forests. Nor your mountains yonder. I am a man of the streets. I like to push through crowds, feel bodies about me. I am a man of the world, not of the wilderness."

Sakim was awake and he was smiling. "I, too, miss the world and the women," he said, "but this. . . this is *new*! It is splendid! It is unknown! What feet have

110

trod this soil? What lungs have breathed this air? What mysteries lie beyond the mountains?"

Rufisco shrugged. "I know what lies beyond your mountains, and it is only more mountains. Beyond each bend in the road there is another bend in the road. You may go, but I shall sit in a tavern and drink the wine of the land, of whatever land, and pinch the girls of the country and perhaps be slapped for my pinching, but smiled at, too.

"You are a merchant, Barnabas, and you, Sakim, a poet. I am a lover. This voyage has convinced me finally. I shall sit somewhere with a glass and throw bread to the pigeons."

I arose. "Very well, but for the present we had best be getting out upon the sound, and wary of the *Jolly Jack*."

"A neat trick," Rufisco commented, "to be seen by the one. . . if it is there. . . and not by the other, which is certainly there."

From the river bank I studied the river. It flowed, brown and muddy, toward the sound. There was nothing upon the water but a great dead tree upon whose bare branches a brown bird perched, in ruffled contentment, accepting the free ride.

We shoved off, and lifting our sail, scudded along before the breeze, our eyes alert for the *Jack*, for floating snags, and for the sound that lay before us where the river's wide mouth ended. Clearing the river mouth finally we turned into the main sound.

Mid-day was past, but no sail lifted against the sky. There were only clouds and gulls, their white wings catching the modest flash of a sullen sun. Far away to the east we thought we could see the coastal banks, yet we saw no mast, no dark hull, only the gray water and behind us the darker green of the shore.

Huddled in the stern I unrolled my charts and gave them study. Two great sounds were here protected from the sea by narrow coastal islands, and into these sounds flowed several rivers, large and small. I believed it was the southermost from which we had come. Several openings through the coastal banks permitted access to the sounds from the sea, and these as well as some of the rivers were mapped in astonishing detail. Obviously someone had explored this coast most carefully, or portions of it, at least.

Through the night we sailed, taking turns at the tiller, the wind holding well. At daybreak it fell off and we dipped and bobbed in a choppy sea, with the dim gray line of dawn off to the northwest.

Visibility was poor, yet we saw no ship. The sun arose and after a while we caught an offshore breeze and worked in closer to the shore, watching for a cove or bay into which we might go for shelter.

It was a low shore when we found it, a swampy place, yet offering shelter. Sakim threw a weighted line ashore and let it wind around a tree, then we hauled in closer. Wading ashore, we made fast with a simple slipknot, knowing well how swiftly we might leave.

We had a little food. We built a fire, ate, and I worked at making arrows for my long-bow.

We saw no savages. A few ducks and geese flew up from time to time, and one of the geese I killed with an arrow. Two of us slept onshore, the other on the boat. We rested, ate, and rested again, and in the evening when I went down to the sea to look for whatever might be seen, I saw a deer and killed it.

So we skinned it out, stretched the hide, and hung the meat for drying, aiding the process with smoke.

We had carried our goods aboard the boat, all but

the meat, and Sakim was taking in our line, waiting for Rufisco and me, ready to shove off.

I heard a cry. . . a choked, hoarse cry.

Turning swiftly I saw Rufisco. There were four arrows in him and a dozen savages rushing toward us. Sakim fired.

A man spun and dropped, but the others were not dismayed by the sound, and came on. I caught up my sword and wheeled about, taking a wide slash as I turned, and severing an uplifted arm holding a tomahawk. Sakim had dropped the one pistol and lifted the fowling piece, which was charged with shot, and fired it into them.

They scattered, two dropped, one of them very bloody, and I rushed in and had Rufisco by the collar. Back I went, sword on guard, dragging him through the water and into the boat, which Sakim shoved off. A flight of arrows, pursued us.

One scratched me, another lodged in my clothing, but Rufisco was aboard, and when they rushed again we were well out of their reach, the wind filling our sail.

Rufisco stared up at me, breathing in hoarse gasps, a bloody froth upon his lips. "Too late!" he mumbled. "There will be no wine with the passing girls, no sitting in the sun."

He was not a man to lie to, and he knew as well as I that with two arrows in his lungs there was little that could be done. He held on to my hand and I could not take it from him to do what might be done to make him easier. Maybe the handclasp was all he wanted at the moment.

"Bury me where I can smell the sea," he said, after spitting blood.

"We can push the arrows through," I said. "They're showing out your back."

One was through his thigh, and bleeding bad.

"Let me be. The knowledge of death was in me." He spat again. "At least, I die with men."

He lay on his side on the gig's bottom, and there was no way I could make him easy without causing more pain. He lay there, eyes closed, breathing hoarsely, always that bloody froth at his lips. I wiped it away.

He opened his eyes again, strangely quiet. "A gray day, that an Italiano should die upon a gray day!"

"We can reach the coastal islands," Sakim said. "There we can find a safe place."

I held his hand with my left, and with my right the tiller. It was a long way across, and somewhere upon the crossing Rufisco died. . . I do not know when, nor even where. Except at the last his fingers held no longer to mine, and I placed the hand down and Sakim looked over at me, but said nothing.

We had lost a comrade, one not easy to lose.

The moon was high when we came up to shore again. It was a long sandy shore on which the surf of the sound rolled up softly.

We beached the gig and carried a line inland to make fast to a low-growing tree. Then we carried the body of Rufisco ashore and above the level of the tide we dug a grave, and there we buried him where he could hear the winds blow, and feel the pulse of the sea. It would not be too different, I thought, than his own Mediterranean, for this too was an inland water, and this too, was warm.

Taking a sight upon a tree, I marked the place for memory, but in the morning, when there was light enough, I carved a name on a slab and placed it there. I knew not the day of his birth, but gave that of his death. His name, too, I placed there, although the place a man leaves is in the hearts of those he leaves behind, and in his work, not upon a slab. . .

We went back to the boat, then, and shoved off, lifting our sail and pointing our bows again to the north. And all that day we saw no sail, nor the next nor the next nor the next.

When again we walked upon land it was on the shores of the northern sound. I killed a deer there, at ninety paces, with one arrow, and we ate well. Later we collected the leaves from a plant Sakim recognized and made a tea, and not a bad one.

We rested on the sand, and Sakim said to me, "It is a good land, this, a fine land." He sat up suddenly. "You should stay in this land, this should be your home."

"Here?" I was not astonished, for the thought had been in me, too. "Perhaps. I would like a family. A man should build. He should always build."

"You want sons?"

"Sons and daughters."

I raised on one elbow. "I wonder about you, Sakim."

"There is no need. I was once almost a philosopher, my friend, but there was too much of the rascal in me. There was also a woman. . . the daughter of a very important man. I was rascal enough to woo her, and philosopher enough to leave quickly when we were discovered."

"Have you never been back?"

"To be killed by soldiers? Or imprisoned? Besides, she was a philosopher, too."

"What do you mean by that?"

"When she saw that I was gone she faced the re-

115

alities and married another man. Now she is rich, important, and domestic. I would no longer be interested in her, and she would only be amused by me."

"You were a student?"

"I was a teacher. My father, my grandfather and my great-grandfather were judges, and so was I to be."

"You were fortunate. I had few books, and no school."

Sakim shrugged. "You had your father, obviously a wise man, and you had a gift."

"I? A gift?"

"A gift of listening. When men spoke, you heard, and of what you heard, you thought." He sat up. "And now," he smiled wickedly, "Oh, Master of Wisdom, we should float our craft. . . We will catch no *Tiger* on this shore."

Our sail was no sooner up, our craft before the wind, than we saw her, broad and beautiful across the way, Captain Brian Tempany's three-master coming down upon us, all sails set and a bone in her teeth, as the saying is.

We hove to and, with Sakim at the tiller, I stood by the mast and waved my hat.

She came along up to us, taking in sail as she approached, and there were faces at the bow rail and aft, and there was Captain Tempany, and Corvino!

Corvino as well, and Jublain. . . good old Jublain!

And then another face. I was startled and blinked my eyes, but it was she. It was Abigail.

Her hair blowing in the wind, smiling at me, her eyes bright with welcome.

"See her, Sakim?" I said, half-turning. "That is why I dream."

"I see, I do indeed. But she is not to dream about, my friend, she *is* the dream!"

116

Chapter 13

An hour later, in the cabin, and over a glass of sack, I explained our situation.

Tempany did not interrupt, only nodding from time to time as he paced the deck. "So we suspected," he said, "but there was no chance. The *Jack* slipped from her moorings and was well down the river before we discovered that you were missing."

He paused. "You have furs, you say?"

"Getting them will not be easy. I am afraid it cannot be done without alerting Bardle. He has you outgunned, Captain."

"Perhaps. And we want no trouble." He frowned. "We should recover your furs, then sail up the coast. There're the Spanish below us." He glanced at me. "What would you suggest?"

"Move now. . . at once. Recover the furs and get away before Bardle is prepared. Once he knows your vessel is in these waters, he will be alert."

Tempany moved to the companionway and called. In a few minutes he returned. "You're sure of the water's depth?"

"We are. . . and Sakim and I will go in after the furs."

He went on deck and Abigail smoothed her skirt with careful hands. "I was dreadfully frightened," she said quietly. "I was afraid something terrible had happened to you."

117

"How do you happen to be here?" I asked.

She laughed. "I convinced him I'd not be safe in London! I think he wanted to bring me, anyway, and all he needed was an excuse."

"Have you been ashore?"

"Oh, no!"

"It's beautiful," I said. "So many kinds of trees, and flowers everywhere. Of course," I added, "there's alligators and bears and Indians."

"We saw some alligators, and once some Indians came out and tried to get us to come ashore. We did not go, although we traded with them for some dried meat and a couple of huge turtles."

"I am glad you came," I said suddenly. "I have been thinking of you."

She glanced at me. "Really? With all those alligators and Indians to think of, I am surprised."

"From alligators and Indians there is always a chance of escape," I said smiling.

"And from me?"

"A much smaller chance, but I am not sure I would try."

Tempany called down the hatch. "Sackett? Come on deck."

He had land on his starb'rd bow. It was the passage from the northern sound to the southern. I stood by him as we started into the passage, for we had passed it before.

"That man you have with you? He's a Moor?"

"Aye, a good man, and an educated one." I told him about Rufisco and the sudden attack by Indians.

"I've been told some are friendly," Tempany commented.

"Some are, but others are as different as Europeans, either as individuals or tribes. We are at war with the

Spanish, or on the verge of it. A ship at sea is in danger from whatever ship it encounters. Indians may be friendly one time, enemies another. They respect strength, and very little else."

When we had passed into the southern sound and saw no sail, we went below, and for the first time in many weeks I sat down to a civilized meal with well-cooked food.

As we ate, I told him of my thoughts of the land. "It is beautiful, and there is nothing in England that surpasses it. I think I may well continue to venture here, to trade with the Indians, perhaps even to buy land from them."

"It is soon," Tempany objected. "It is too soon. A fancied slight can turn them against you. I have no dealings with these Indians, as they are called, but I have dealt with others of a similar kind, and they are easily offended. One can create trouble through misunderstanding, for their ways are different than ours."

"Granted. . . but I shall learn."

"You had best come back to England first," Tempany said, "there is the matter of a gentleman who would make you his heir. And no small thing it is."

For a moment I was silent. How to tell him the spell those empty rivers had cast upon me? Or the vastness of that land out there? The mystery of it?

"I must go beyond the mountains," I said.

"There are always mountains," Tempany said grimly, "of one kind or another. Think, before you decide. What future is there here but a life among savages, until you become savage yourself?

Later, Jublain and Corvino were waiting on deck. "We have traded a little along the coast," Corvino said, "and we have done well."

They had already met Sakim, and the three were friends. I gave a thought to Rufisco, buried under the sand. He wanted the sun, and the wine and the girls. I would drink a toast to him, someday, in some such place as that of which he dreamed.

"Sakim! You have done many things, but have you ever built a ship?"

"I have. And several I have rebuilt after battle or storm." He looked at me thoughtfully. "You are thinking of a ship?"

"I am. . . and a cargo of potash."

"Potash?"

"It's used in making glass, and soap, too. I shall burn oak wood, perhaps some other hardwoods as well. Leach the ashes and ship them to England."

"They will pay for that?" Jublain was skeptical.

"Aye," Corvino said. "A glassmaker would pay ten shillings per hundredweight, and here there are forests of oaks. All it takes is work."

"I am a warrior," Jublain said contemptuously.

"And a poor one," Corvino agreed. "A warrior who will not soil his hands, but does not have a bit for wine or ale? Or one who works a little and buys what ale and wine he needs?"

"If it comes to that," Jublain admitted.

The weather was fair and the wind held steady. The three-master moved along smoothly, yet slowed by the current, and when we were abeam of the rocks, Sakim, Jublain and I shoved off in the gig, which had been towed astern. It needed only a short time to retrieve our first cache of furs, load them into the gig and start back. There was no sign of Nick Bardle or his crew, nor of any Indians.

We moved upstream to the mouth of the first branching stream of size. There we put the wheel over and, using great care, let the current strike our starb'rd bow and slowly swing the ship around. There was room enough and to spare, and when we had turned we started downstream, moving toward the farther bank.

The low island to which we came looked no different than it had. I went down the ladder into the gig, followed by Sakim and Jublain again, and once more we pushed away from the *Tiger*'s side toward familiar land.

Despite our previous visit, it was no easy thing to find the hulk again, and a slow, burdensome task to carry the furs all the way to the gig. Yet carry them we did, and again we pushed off. At the *Tiger*, Sakim climbed aboard and the furs were hoisted.

Suddenly, there were shouts from above, frantic cries, then the boom of a cannon. The *Jolly Jack* had rounded the bend. A shot struck the water nearby and as the sails went up on the *Tiger* the wind caught them and she gave a lurch, turning quickly and thrusting sharply forward.

As her bows thrust forward, she bumped hard against the gig. Standing in its bow, having just made fast the towline, I was pitched headfirst into the water.

I went down, down, down. My lungs struggled for breath, my hands lashed at the water and I shot up. The gig, trailing behind the *Tiger* now, was a good dozen feet away. I heard the boom of another cannon and saw the *Jolly Jack* closing, yet there was a sudden concussion, a nearer shot, and I saw the ball hit the rail of the *Jack* and throw splinters high into the air.

There was a scream, then the *Tiger*, firing at will, let go with another. The *Jack*, heading upstream then, passed the *Tiger* and I could see men racing along the deck to bring the stern gun to bear.

Treading water, I suddenly, realized the *Jolly Jack* was abreast of me and not fifty yards off. The *Tiger* was sailing away. Instantly, I dove, swimming under water toward the island. Reaching its shore I walked and crawled until almost out of water. Then, with my face exposed, I lay still.

The *Jack* was turning about to give chase.

I could see confusion on her decks, one gun dismounted, a portion of the rail shot away. What damage had been done the *Tiger*, I had no idea.

When she was well past I crawled on my belly up the sand, trying to imitate the wriggling of an alligator. When I came near some brush I crawled in. There, I sat up and looked slowly around.

I sat amid some low-growing brush on a sandpit on the island of the hulk. I had only the clothes in which I stood, my sword and dagger, nothing more.

Obviously the *Jolly Jack* had been lying in wait in some inlet, her mast lost among treetops, and we too intent upon my sandy island and the furs to spot her. Now the *Jack* was in hot pursuit and that she was the faster of the two vessels I knew full well. Also, she was heavier-gunned, heavier-manned, and altogether a more complete fighting ship.

The *Tiger* had a lead and it had the wind. There was nothing for it but to run, and the *Jack* would follow.

And I?

I would remain here, on this island . . . alone.

Chapter 14

When the *Jolly Jack* was well away I got slowly to my feet. I was dripping wet and clammy. The air seemed to have grown colder with a wind from off the sea. From my charts, the growth about me, and the season, this should be southern land, yet nobody had told the wind.

I went to the old hulk, almost buried in sand, and went in under her side. Well I knew how to build a fire with bow and string, yet work as I might this time no flame would come. At last, too cold and weary to try more, I dug a place for myself in the sand, filled it with grass and crawled down inside it to sleep. And sleep I did . . . sword in hand.

Dawn broke cold with another spitting rain. My shirt and breeches had dried but little. Back under the hulk I found a bird's nest of twigs, dried grass and hair. This I brought out and once more set to work with bow and string.

Soon a tiny tendril of smoke arose, and I glimpsed a spark. I blew gently . . . it went out. I worked again, worked until my palms were sore, and then again the smoke. I worked harder and harder, and soon a spark . . . another! I blew gently, ever so gently. The spark brightened, dimmed, brightened again as I breathed upon it, and a tendril of dry grass began to smoke. Soon I had a fire, a very small fire.

When it was burning, I crept outside and looked carefully around.

Where was the *Tiger?* Had she escaped? Or been taken by the *Jolly Jack?* Had I been seen after I fell into the river? Did they guess that I lived?

There was fuel enough and more, but, sitting by the fire, I was suddenly overcome by depression.

I was alone. Even if the *Tiger* survived, it might be too severely injured to return for me, even if Captain Tempany believed in my survival.

They were gone, and I was alone. What happened now was up to me.

The old hull in which I sheltered myself had somehow been destroyed, its crew drowned or killed by Indians, the hull finally beached here on this island. It had been as large a vessel as the *Tiger.* There was little upon which to make an estimate, but the line of the bow was unusual. It did not appear to have broken in half, only that the larger portion was buried in sand, many years ago.

I went outside into the rain and dragged some brush nearer, then picked up various odds and ends of logs, broken timbers and the like to keep my fire alive.

The hull was thick, and exposure to the elements had not weakened it, I could wish for no better shelter. At the back end I could go into what must have been a sort of forecastle, but that I had not yet explored.

What we had first assumed was the captain's quarters was nothing of the kind, and I was determined, when time permitted, to explore further. Perhaps even to dig a little.

When time permitted! And what kind of time would I have now? Merely enough to keep soul and body together, to eke out a precarious living. That would take all the time and skill I had.

First, I must have food. I must make another bow and some arrows, and I must get skins for a warmer jacket, for now I stood in nothing but breeches and shirt, neither of which would last. In the meantime I had to eat.

Several times along the river I had seen great turtles; I saw none now. Several times I had seen deer, but I saw none. Fishing in such weather as this was out of the question.

The channel between my island and the far shore was not wide, but the current ran swiftly. I was a good swimmer, but not that good, and had no wish to trust myself to that powerful current with a sword to impede my movements. So I added sticks to the fire and huddled close, trying to envelop it and absorb all the heat I could.

But to sit idle was impossible, so I searched among the rubble of drift around the old hulk until I found a long, straight shaft of about seven feet in length, and sharpening the end with my dagger, I hardened the point in the fire. It balanced well, would make a staff for walking, and a crude spear. Yet it was in no sense an adequate weapon.

Reeds and willows there were in profusion, so I'd have no trouble about arrow shafts. Points were another thing, and points needed time. I'd also need a bow. In the meanwhile there was a thing I could do, and with those willows closest to hand. I could make a fish-trap.

Slipping out into the rain, I hurriedly cut a couple of dozen long whips of willow. Forming a hoop of one of these I began to bind the ends of the others to the hoop at intervals, using willow bark or the fibres of some of the coarse grass growing nearby to make them fast. Stretching them out, I then bound the other ends together in a tight group making a sort of elongated funnel.

With some much shorter sticks tied to a half circle of willow, I formed a sort of trap to put at the opening. The current and movements of the fish itself would allow them to enter; getting out would, hopefully, be much more difficult. It was crude, hurriedly done, and not a job I would have boasted of to any fen-man, but I was hungry and anxious. When the trap was completed I waded waist-deep into the water and moored it with stakes. Returning I found patches of scurvy grass, known as useful in preventing scurvy. Tearing up a handful I returned wet and cold to my shelter, huddled over the fire and ate the grass.

It was mightily unsatisfactory.

I was lonesome and tired. Shivering, I huddled over the fire, getting up at intervals to drag fuel closer to hand, for the fire was insatiable. Small though I kept it, its angry flames ate hungrily of the wood, and I dared not use the greener, slower burning wood which would produce too much smoke.

Finally, I napped.

Suddenly I was awake. It was dusk. My fire was smoldering coals. For a moment I lay still, staring at two of those coals. Somehow they were out beyond the edge of my fire. What would coals be doing out there? How would——?

I came off the sand with a lunge, narrowly missing banging my skull against the over-hanging ship's side. With a sweep of a hand I knocked some stacked wood into the flames, the smaller stuff gathered for kindling in case my fire went out.

The fire sputtered, then the flames reached up, and my hand went out, grasping for my spear.

Facing me, just beyond the fire, was an alligator. Perhaps a crocodile, for I did not know one from the other. Its small red eyes gleamed from the fire's reflection, and I crouched. I yelled at it, but it paid no attention, its eyes fixed on mine with a baleful gleam.

Escape was out of the question. To go to right or left would still leave me within sweep of the mighty tail, and I had been warned many times that the alligator strives to knock its prey into the water or break its legs with its tail. The jaws were parted slightly revealing rows of ugly teeth, and hanging from them the remains of some other creature it had eaten, or perhaps only some riverweed.

There were no rocks. I threw a handful of sand, but the beast paid no attention. His tail moved slightly. Once he lifted a foot as if to move, then put it down again.

I added a heavier stick to the fire, suddenly awake that my fuel supply was badly depleted. And when my fuel was gone? How could I face such a monster with my six foot stick? True, I had my sword, but how tough was the hide? This alligator was a monster.

Moving slightly to one side, his eyes and nose followed me, the jaws parting slightly as if in anticipation.

Suddenly he lunged toward me and I thrust hard at his eye with my spear. It missed, but the jolt of the blow against the horny plate jarred my arm to the elbow. I had heard of natives wrestling these creatures, but surely their creatures had been smaller than mine—as large around in the body as a good-sized donkey.

He came a tentative foot further, in no way disturbed by my spear. He was crowding me, knowing I was trapped, knowing that if he could force me deeper into my shell I would be helpless. He avoided the fire, coming at me around the right side, moving carefully.

I stabbed with the spear, ineffectually, then thrust suddenly with my sword. The point of the blade took him above the nose and skidded along the upper side of his jaw, making a long scratch, but penetrating scarcely at all.

He came on, a step further, circling the fire, jaws agape. I was bent over now, unable to move swiftly, still near the fire but being inexorably backed into the old hull. I struck again with my spear but suddenly the jaws snapped and the spear was gone, broken in half. Sword in hand, I thrust suddenly. The point penetrated an inch, perhaps more. Instantly withdrawing I cut a slash at the ugly nose. The jaws gaped, and with incredible swiftness the alligator lunged.

He was a huge fellow, his body twelve to fifteen feet long, and when he lunged he must have come forward at least six feet. I twisted under the overhang, trying to get outside. My foot slipped in the sand and I fell, my left hand falling near the fire.

As the monster started for me, my hand closed over the end of the heavy stick I had recently put into the fire. Its end was aflame, and I hurled it with all my strength into the gaping maw before me.

The beast gave a tremendous roar and went into a convulsion, twisting this way and that in a fury of pain and anger.

Rolling over into the edge of the fire, I sprang up and dove out into the rain, stumbled and fell, got up again, and was knocked sprawling by the monster, rushing for the river oblivious of me. I heard him splash, saw him submerge. He surfaced almost at once with a roar, then went down again.

For a long time I lay still, sprawled on the sand. Thunder rumbled in the distance, and slowly, I drew my hands under me. Somehow I still clung to my sword. Getting up I looked around, rain streaming down my face, soaking my clothes once more.

Staggering, I made for my shelter in the hulk. Once out of the rain, I fell on on the churned up sand and lay there, gasping and trembling. Finally, I pulled myself together.

My fire had been scattered, but here and there some embers smouldered and using a stick for a rake, I gathered them together and added fuel. The fuel I now had was wet, but slowly the fire took hold. I crouched beside it, trembling.

There could be no thought of sleep. I gathered fuel, and sword across my knees, I dozed and waited for the dawn that seemed never to come. And when it came at last it was gray and cold with a wind blowing the rain before it, bending the trees, and whipping sand like shot that rattled against the hulk and stung my cheeks.

Sword in hand, for now I expected danger behind every bush, I went down the island to where I thought I had seen some green ash trees. They were there, and I cut a long, smooth pole about the size of my wrist or a bit larger. It was a young tree that had been fire-killed, and looked to be a proper bit of bow material.

Taking it back to the hulk, I picked up several fist-sized pieces of rock on the return journey. Seated once more beside my fire, I began working to smooth down my bow and shape it to my thinking. It was a slow, painstaking task, but it helped to keep me warm, and a bow I must have if I was to live.

Later, again with sword in hand, I went to my fish-trap. It was there . . . a part of it. Something, possibly an alligator, had destroyed it to get at the fish it had undoubtedly held.

I swore bitterly, then taking what fragments might be used, I went back to the hulk to do the job once more. It was almost dusk when I replanted the trap and returned to my shelter to resume work on the bow, flattening the inner side, rounding the outer.

I felt near to starving.

That night I built my fire larger and slept fitfully, awakening to add fuel to the flames, sometimes to peer out into the darkness. My fire was well hidden and I had small fear it would be seen from the mainland.

At daybreak I went to my fish trap and it held three fine, large fish!

Rolling them in clay at the river's edge, I carried them back to camp and buried them in coals at the fire's edge. Later, when I could wait no longer, I ate them . . . all three, and they were delicious.

During the night the rain ceased so I kept my fire still smaller. Then I rigged a couple of deadfalls, took another fish from my trap, and ate some more scurvy grass.

My next move must be to the mainland, to escape from my island prison. Twice I went out to the highest place on the island and stood among the trees looking down river. I saw nothing, no movement, no sail.

On the fourth day I completed my bow and several arrows, and on the fifth day I found a huge, old dead tree clinging to some brush at the island's edge. If I could straddle that, shove off and hit that point yonder . . .

On the sixth day, with two smoked fish inside my shirt for rations, I shoved off, and in less than a half an hour was afoot in the mainland woods.

My safest bet was to go to Potaka, yet I had no more faith in his protection than had Rufisco, so I struck out overland, for the coast.

And on the morning of the seventh day, I killed a deer.

Chapter 15

Crouching in the low brush that crowned the sand hills where I waited, I studied the shore line with infinite patience. Already my eyes had scanned the sound, and no sail showed itself against the blue water, nor the blue sky beyond, nor close in against the sand.

From time to time I had seen the tracks of Indians, but I had seen neither man, woman, nor child. I had eaten well of my venison, and had some still with me. There were well-used trails here and there but I avoided them, keeping to smaller trails or to the woods themselves.

Travel was slower, yet it served me well, for I was

learning more about the trees, the life of the forest, and what it was that lay before me.

I must assume I would be some time ashore. If the *Tiger* had escaped, it might come back . . . and might not. If it had been taken by the *Jolly Jack*, I would be unlikely to see any of my friends again. The thought of Abigail in the hands of Nick Bardle was intolerable.

The *Jack* would return. Perhaps the *Tiger* also. These sounds were relatively secure against the worst of the storms. Undoubtedly all these waters could be frightening in stormy weather. But the banks interposed a wall between a ship and the sea, and there were numerous inlets and river mouths that offered shelter.

Bardle was a cold fish . . . a careful man. He would see the advantages of the sounds. In the meantime, I must live, and if possible accumulate more furs.

With deadfall traps I snared a few animals: several mink, an otter, four beaver, and with an arrow I killed a fox.

That night the traps I set brought me another fox, a mink, and a rabbit. I skinned out the first two, ate the third, and at daybreak was working my way through the sandhills toward one hill, taller than most, from which I hoped to have a view of the sound.

Coming through the brush, I stumbled upon a path, a well-used path. and my first glance brought me up standing. There in the path, clear-cut and sharp, was a heel print! No moccasin, but a small boot, perfectly-shaped and not worn.

Astonished, I glanced right and left, saw nothing, and began a study of the trail.

The wearer of the small boot had come along the trail from between the sandhills, and not longer ago than last night or the afternoon before. She had been accompanied by at least two men.

She?

It was a small print, a very small boot, and it must be a woman's. Yet I knew of no woman, not an Indian, in this part of the world but . . .

Abigail!

Smoke . . . I smelled smoke. A moment later I glimpsed their camp. There were three men and Abigail.

She sat across the fire from me and I was proud of her. No downcast face, no sloping shoulders, no look of defeat. She held her head up. "You will be hung in chains," she was saying, and her manner was assured. "You do not realize what you have done."

Darkling was there, he was one of them, and he was a hard man. "You're a simple fool," he said roughly. "Who is to know what happens here? You're ours, to do with as we choose. We'll have Tempany himself before dark. Not a prisoner mind you, but dead. We've no time for prisoners . . . unless they are young and pretty.

"We have to decide." He glanced at the others. "Do we take her back to the others? Or keep her here for awhile?"

At that moment I stood up directly opposite her, and she saw me at once. I wasted no time on politeness or warnings. These were evil men and I well knew it. I loosed an arrow at the man nearest Darkling, a swarthy, muscular fellow who looked to be the most dangerous.

The distance was not over fifteen yards, if so much, and the arrow shot true.

133

It went through him about six inches above his great brass belt-buckle, and he gave a grunt and grabbed it with both hands, then went to his knees.

The others turned sharply, but I had dropped down, another arrow notched and ready. Someone shot, far to the right, for my target had half-turned after taking the arrow, giving a false impression of its origin.

My second arrow was less successful, for it struck a great bone-button on the man's coat. One saw few buttons and I had no use for them, and less now. The arrow glanced upward, inflicting a minor scratch on the man's face, and then they saw me.

Both men came out with their blades and they started for me. Abigail—bless her—gathered her skirts and fled into the brush.

Managing a longbow in that brush was not easy, so I tried no more shots, nor did I intend to fight. I simply fled as she had done, circling to intercept her, which I soon did. I could hear them crashing in the brush, but they were off the point. Catching Abigail by the hand, we ran a weaving route through the trees and to my sandhill.

There was a deep cut in that dune made by some water cutting a way down where a tree's roots had left a gaping hole. We climbed to the hill's top, hidden as it was, and sat down on a great log.

"I must say," Abigail said, "you took long enough!"

"Long enough?" I stared at her dumbfounded.

"Well," she smoothed her skirt with both hands, "if a man is going to rescue a lady he should have done it sooner, but thank you, nonetheless. I am obliged."

"Where is the *Tiger?*"

"On the sand not far from here. That awful Captain Bardle hulled her twice and shot away our fore-mast. Several of the men have been killed and all were scattered."

"Captain Tempany?"

"He's kept some of them together! I was going to join him with Lila. She turned back to the ship to get something she had forgotten, and while I waited these men rushed from the trees and captured me."

We had a good view and for the moment we were safe.

I could barely make out the *Tiger* through the trees. She was hard aground, no mistaking that, and her foremast was down, trailing over her side. When I moved away a little to get a better view, I could see no movement near her. Nor was there any sign of the *Jolly Jack*.

"I think we had best remain," I suggested, "until matters settle down a bit. From here we can see all about and can choose our way when we leave."

She glanced at the bow. "Where did you get that?"

"I made it. It isn't very good, but I was hungry and in a hurry."

"I think it does very well. I could have cheered when you shot that man." She glanced at me. "We are going to have a bad time, aren't we?"

I shrugged, watching the beach and the slope to the beach. "She doesn't look too badly hurt," I nodded to indicate the *Tiger*, "so we may be able to float her again."

Pacing about I studied all the approaches to our sandhill. It appeared to offer so little in the way of shelter that I doubted they would come hence, yet if they wished to see about——

"I am very tired," Abigail said suddenly. "Would you think me ungrateful if I slept?"

"You'd be wise," I said bluntly. "My father was a soldier and he always told me a good soldier never stood when he could sit, and never sat when he could lie down, and ate whenever there was food."

I showed her a place near a log where leaves had thickly gathered. It was a shadowed place and still. I picked up broken branches from the leaves and smoothed them for her, and when she lay down she went at once to sleep. Would that I could lie down and sleep so easily!

I peered at the woods below. After a while I found several straight, light branches and commenced to work on them with an edge of stone to make more arrows for the crude quiver I had shaped from bark.

Suddenly a knowledge came upon me. I would take my furs and return to England. But I would gather about me a few trusty souls and return again. This was the land!

Yet there was a shadow across my return. Rupert Genester would be there, awaiting me.

Well, he need not wait. I would seek him out, and have done with it once and for all.

I must find Captain Tempany and we must prepare to assert ourselves. We must rear a defensible position and we must repair and refloat, if possible, the *Tiger*. If not, but one thing remained.

Take the *Jolly Jack*.

It would serve Nick Bardle right to be left ashore, then. My eyes went again to the *Tiger*. The three-master was well aground, but aside from the fallen mast seemed to be damaged but little. It had been hulled twice, Abigail said. Yet the holes might be patched.

My furs should still be aboard her, and some of my trade goods.

Abigail was stirring when I next looked at her, and then her eyes opened. She looked at me, startled, then gradually came awake. She sat up. Automatically her hands went to her hair. "Barnabas!" It was, I believed, the first time she had called me that. "What shall we do?"

"Go down to the *Tiger*," I said.

"The *Tiger!* But they will find us there!"

"We do nothing here. Sooner or later Captain Tempany will come back to his ship. We shall be there and ready."

"And if Nick Bardle comes first?"

"We shall prepare to receive him. I have no time to waste dodging him, nor do I intend to. He has cost me dearly already, but next time he shall pay."

Late afternoon came across the sound leaving an edging of silver on the sand behind it, dusk crept up the hills and erased the last vestiges of color from the tops of the old trees. And when the last shadow was gone, we went down from the mountain and across the beach to the vessel.

Aft, where she lay in water, a rope ladder trailed down. Sheathing my sword, a dagger in my teeth, I went up and aboard, ready for what might come. All was dark and still.

Abigail followed after, doing remarkably well on the ladder and over the rail, despite her skirts. Aft we went to the cabin, and all was dark and quiet. Over the stern lights I hung a heavy blanket from the bed, and then cautiously, with flint and steel, a light.

All was in turmoil. What I looked for was a pistol, and finding one, I charged it. What Abigail looked for was clothing, and she found it.

"I want to change," she said, looking at me.

"Change then," I replied, "but quickly." Stepping

out I closed the door behind me, then went into the smaller mate's quarters and felt about for the hasp of the gunlocker. It was intact.

Apparently Bardle had been too intent on pursuit of Tempany to loot the *Tiger*, or believed it safely within his hands, with no need for hurry.

Breaking the hasp with an axe from a nearby bulkhead, I took out a musket, another pistol, and charged both. On the after rail was mounted a swivel-gun, and I charged it also. It could cover a large part of the beach from the high side of the vessel. The *Tiger* was canted slightly to the starb'rd side, and the swivel-gun, mounted on the port rail, had an excellent field of fire.

From the galley I brought food to the cabin, knocked, and was admitted. Abigail looked lovely in a simple gray dress with white cuffs and collar. She had made up a small bundle of whatever she might need, and stood ready for leaving.

There was ham, ship's bread, some onions and a bit of dried fruit from the master's mess. Taking a careful look around from the ship's deck, I then joined Abigail in the cabin where we sat to table and ate. We were hungry, and it pleased me mightily to see the hungry way in which Abigail sank her dainty teeth into a bit of ham I'd sliced for her.

I pulled a draught of ale for each, and with mine in one hand and a chunk of ham in the other, I returned to the deck. The beach was empty so far as I could see, but it was growing quite dark. Going below once more, I sat down and finished the best meal I'd had in days, and then began to pack a sack with food to be taken if time and circumstance allowed.

"We are going now?" she asked, watching me pack the sack.

There was reluctance in her tone, and I understood why.

"Not tonight," I said, "unless we must. Do you sleep now, in a good bunk. Tomorrow we will think of going."

"And you?"

"I'll watch," I said. "Be off with you now."

She left, and the door closed gently behind her. I peered out into the darkness from near the swivel-gun. I knew how tired she must be, for I was also tired.

I leaned on the rail and my muscles cried out for me to lie down . . . for a minute only.

There was no sound but the rustle of surf on the sand. Search the woods as I might, I could see no gleam of fire, nor could I hear any sound. It was very still.

Chapter 16

My eyes closed. Almost at once they were open and I felt fear go through me like a shaft of steel, cold and bitter.

To sleep might be to die. More than that, I would leave her whom . . . I hesitated at what I suddenly thought . . . *whom I loved.*

There . . . the thought was complete. But was it

so? Did I love Abigail Tempany? And if so, why? A lovely girl, gentle enough yet with courage and more strength than one would suspect. A lady, but a bright one—she was intelligent, with a good measure of common sense, and the two are not always one.

Now I was awake. For the moment at least my weariness disappeared in contemplation of this new thought. *I was in love.* Yet why should Abigail Tempany, of all people, love me?

Not that she did, of course. There was no reason for it. Why should anybody love me? I was a somewhat ordinary man with ordinary impulses, and some measure of ambition, but I had little, I was less.

Yet I would be something . . . that I knew.

I loved a lady, a fair lady. I wished she were mine in one breath and was glad she was not in a second, for where could I take such a lady? To a cottage in the fens? Abigail? Even if she would consider it, I would not. Would I have her offer slop to pigs and bake eels?

I loved a lady, and a lady must live as a lady deserves.

Well, what was it Jublain had said? I had a sword. Indeed I had, and with a sword a man might win a kingdom, might hold that kingdom against all who came—and might also lose his head for trying.

Suddenly something bumped the hull . . . bumped again. I lifted the sword. I heard the slap of bare feet on the deck, then more feet.

A voice spoke. "There be naught aboard, Cap'n. She's still as death she is, and nobody's taken the hatches off her. What was there is still there."

"Get off that ladder!" It was Nick Bardle's voice. "I am coming aboard."

There was a solid dark cluster of them where the

140

rope ladder hung, and I turned the swivel on them with great good cheer.

"Here's a bit of something for yourself, Cap'n!" I shouted, and fired the swivel.

She belched a solid blast of flame and I heard the thud of the shot as it struck, and a scream. Then I upped with a pistol and let go at a shadow that separated itself from the others, and then another blast from my second pistol and suddenly a third, and this from the cabin door.

Abigail, bless her!

Then with a wild yell from my throat, I went along the deck and at them. I knew not how many they were, nor they how many were here. My swinging blade cut this way and that, a scream, a cry, a clang of metal on metal, and then they were all about me and I was fighting for my life.

Suddenly from below there was a rush of feet, and another cry, and somebody yelled out, "Who's that? Who is that, damn them to hell?"

Somebody was also attacking from below, so I was not alone. Not yet, at least. I parried a blade, thrust, stepped back and with a toe kicked a block in the way of my opponent who spilled over it to hands and knees. If he came up from that—I flicked my blade sidewise and down in a quick gesture—up from that he'd have to fasten his head on again.

Somebody leaped the rail to escape, and another gun flamed beside me. There was Abigail, hair wild about her shoulders in that fleeting glimpse, but aiming with another pistol, and God knows where she found them or how she had charged them.

A man loomed at the head of the ladder and my thrust took him at the base of the throat and lifted. If he lived, that one, he'd truly have a cleft chin.

There was another sound of running feet, a blast or two from below, and then a jumble of voices among which I detected Brian Tempany's.

"Welcome aboard, Cap'n," I said cheerfully, "but do you step carefully. I think they've left some'at behind."

"Is it you, Sackett?"

"Aye, and pleased to see you, and at my side is a lady who shoots uncommon well."

She was there, close against my elbow, her head just a jot above my shoulder. "And how did you come to be awake?"

"I never slept," she said, "for I could see you were heavy with sleep, and was hopeful you'd sleep, for well you should have."

"And I stayed awake for you," I said.

Tempany came over the rail. Dim his face was, in the vague light of a dawn not far away. "I thought you two were dead," he spoke quietly, "I thought Bardle had killed you."

Jublain was at my elbow. "Are you well, then? You've not taken a cutting?"

"Well, aye," I said, "but you shall find some about who are not."

"Four dead on the deck," Corvino said with satisfaction, "and one who fell overside. And there were three done in by us when we closed, and before they broke. I've a feeling there's a few who will carry scars, if they live."

"Sakim?"

"I am here, my friend. A little used, but here."

"Come," Tempany said, "we'll go below. Courtney, you and Fitzpatrick stay on deck. I'll send a tot of rum for each. The rest of you below for what is coming to you.

"Sackett," he turned to me, "come to the cabin. We've much to talk about."

I sheathed my sword, and turned, staggering a little from the onset of weariness now that it was over, or seemed to be. A hand steadied me. "I am beside you, Barnabas, but not strong enough to hold you if you fall, so please stand up!"

Abigail went into her cubbyhole of a cabin.

Tempany had lighted a lantern. We stepped into the cabin. He took up a bottle and two glasses, and then he looked at me under his brows. "Rum? Or no rum? You refused it before."

"This once," I said, "to revive the spirit."

"Ah, we won't talk of that. Your spirit seems in excellent shape, man. And there're a few things for us to discuss, even tonight."

He paused, tasted his rum, then tossed it off, neat and quick. He swallowed, looked at me and put his glass down. "Have you looked at her?"

"At Abigail?" I said.

"No, damn it, at the ship. Have you seen her by day?"

"I have."

"Do you think she'll float again?"

"I do, but if I am wrong there's the *Jack*."

"The *what*?"

"We can take the *Jolly Jack*. She's a good sailer and well-armed, and she deserves better than that lot aboard her now."

"That would be difficult and dangerous," he said, after awhile. "Let us have a look at the *Tiger*."

Yet it was sleep I needed, and I said as much. Reluctantly, he agreed, and when I had stretched out on a settee in the cabin, he went on deck. Obviously if the *Tiger* could be saved, he intended to save it.

I slept, and dreamed of the purple mountains I'd glimpsed far off in the distance when up the river. Those mountains haunted me, and why I knew not. When my eyes opened next, the day was well along and I could smell ham being cooked, and a sound of rustling around in the galley.

For a few minutes I lay still. My mind was filled with the substance of the dream. Somehow, come what may, I must see those mountains. I must walk their trails, know them. Somehow all that was England had faded until it was difficult to even recognize faces I used to know, I could not bring them to memory. I sat up and pulled on my boots, buckled on my sword, then stood for a moment, peering through the parted curtain of the stern lights.

The water was choppy, but not rough. The sky was overcast. I went out on deck, and the first to greet me was Jublain.

"Tempany says you have some idea of taking the *Jack?*"

"If we need her." I glanced toward the beach and the trees and sandhills beyond. Nothing moved.

"It's a bad lot aboard there. A bad, bad lot, but they can fight."

"We'd have to get most of them ashore," I suggested.

Tempany came over the rail. "We can float her," he said, "and the holes can be patched well enough, though there's a deal of work to be done."

He brushed salt from his hands. "What's it like inland, Sackett? Is there land worth having?"

"Some of the fairest I've seen. There's game in plenty, and cattle would thrive here, or pigs or sheep. Tempany," I looked around at him, across my shoulder, "a man could become wealthy here."

"What of the Indians?"

"They war much with each other, so one could not be friends with all, and a man must step carefully to learn of their ways, which be different than ours. But with a good stockade and a few swivel guns a man could protect himself while trying to deal fairly."

Food was brought to the cabin table, and I ate, and well, yet there was more to worry me, for I knew that Nick Bardle, a revengeful man, was still alive.

We needed a forem'st, so with Jublain, Corvino, and Sakim and several of Tempany's men, I led the way into the woods to where some likely mast timber could be found. While they felled the tree, I looked about, marking various trees for future falling, and studying the land for a likely spot for a trading station.

It must be on the river, in a position easily defended, with timber available and a spring if possible.

We floated our tree down river and guided it about to the position of the *Tiger*. All went well, and we saw nothing of Bardle nor his men, nor of the *Jolly Jack*.

Meanwhile we dug out around the hull, using lines and poles to get her on an even keel. We were under no false notions about Bardle. He not only wanted our ship and cargo. He also wanted us . . . dead!

We shifted two guns to the stern that could be brought to bear if an enemy approached us from the waterside, as we more than half expected.

Meanwhile, I saw Abigail only at intervals.

Four days we labored, patching the hull, re-stepping the mast, repairing rigging. I had much experience with splicing line, so could do my share, and did it.

We hoped to float free at an early hightide, yet I had an idea that Bardle was also thinking of tides.

Jublain sat in the cabin with us, his dark, cynical face bored with our talk. "Bardle knows about tides," he said at last, "he knows all that we know, and the man's no fool. Why do you suppose he has done nothing?"

"We served him well on his last attempt," Corvino replied. "He's had his belly full."

Jublain snorted his disgust. "He waits for you to complete repairs," he said. "He wants no hulk on the beach, but a vessel afloat and loaded with cargo he can trade or sell. He has twice or three times the men we have, and he'll come when he wills."

Out upon deck I looked at the sky. Clouds bulked large, and the wind lifted, rustling the rigging, flapping a loose corner of canvas. There was a spatter of heavy drops.

A storm was coming, but storm or not we must use the tide when it came, and with luck we might float free. Brian Tempany came out on deck, glanced at the sky and around, then ordered his men to clean up what tools remained, to get them aboard and make all fast.

"In the storm," I said, "we might slip away."

"We'll ride out the storm," Tempany said, "and leave when it has blown away. I think we'll have our chance then."

Abigail came on deck. The wind was whipping her skirt about her legs, and I braced myself against it, wishing I were warmer dressed.

"Barnabas Sackett," she said. "It is a good name."

"A name is what a man makes it," I said. "My father did well with his and I hope to do as much. The times are changing, and many people are restless with the desire to better themselves. We have too many gentlemen who do nothing, are nothing, and many a yeoman or apprentice with ability who would rise in position if the chance existed." I waved a hand. "Here there is no such restriction."

"Perhaps. But when enough people come here, it will be the same. . . ."

I grinned cheerfully. "Then the secret is to come first and help to make the rules by which the rest will live."

"The King will do that," she objected.

"No doubt. But the King is far away, and his word needs time in which to travel, and men have a way of making their own adjustments. There is no Court here, hence no need for courtiers. There is great need for strength, courage and intelligence, and you will find those qualities as often or more among artisans as gentlemen."

"You like this?" she indicated the shore.

My eyes swept the coastline, green and lovely even under the sullen clouds. "I do. It is a magnificent coast, a land filled with everything. I shall go away. But I shall come back again."

She looked at me for a long time, and what she might have said then I do not know, for Captain Tempany emerged from the companionway shouting, "Stand by, fore-and-aft! The tide's coming in!"

Even as he spoke, a wave of water rolled past the hull, out past the bow, then receded slowly, carrying away some of the sand with it.

"Here she comes!" Jublain shouted. "Sail, ho!"

It was the *Jolly Jack*, carrying a good stand of sail, coming down toward us.

Chapter 17

She was yet some distance off and the wind was wrong for her, but that she intended to come up to us for an attack was obvious. And there we lay, still aground, with only a few small guns to bear.

It was my time to act, and I acted now, without thinking, without speaking to Tempany.

"Sakim! Jublain! Corvino! Here . . . to me!" I grabbed a passing sailor and shoved him toward a gun. "Get a sling around it. Quick now!"

Sakim had come running and I directed him to haul our gig alongside and get into it. Running to the cabin I retrieved my longbow and the arrows I had made as well as some I had brought from England.

"Tumble in," I told Sakim. "We'll do a bit of business this day!"

From the deck they lowered down a light but powerful cast-iron gun and we lashed it into place. The gig was light and fast, under ordinary conditions, but now she sat deep and we shifted what weight there was to counterbalance the gun. Then we pushed off, got our sail up and headed for the open sound, needing all the room we could get.

The tide was rising rapidly, but it needed time to float such a craft as the *Tiger*, although glancing back I could see that Tempany had a boat out astern of her with a line to the ship and the boats crew pulling with a will.

If the *Jolly Jack* had sighted our gig, she seemed to think it of no importance. It was the *Tiger* they wanted, and they wanted her free of the sand and their work done for them. The *Jack* was moving in toward the coast now, prepared to stand off and demand a surrender or shell the *Tiger* to bits.

Now we put about our gig and commenced moving toward the *Jack*. My thought was to cause trouble, to buy time for the *Tiger* to get well afloat, and what I proposed to do was the height of foolishness. All depended on the maneuverability of the gig, much of which had been sacrificed to carry the cannon.

We edged in close and intent upon the *Jack*. They paid us small attention. We laid our gun on the form'st and touched a match to the hole.

A moment only, then our gun boomed and the gig jerked violently in the water. There was a startled shout from the *Jack*, then an angry voice telling us to sheer off or be sunk.

We had done no harm to the mast, but we had hit the bulwark just forward of mast, carried away some rigging made fast there and scattered fragments of wood in all directions.

Carefully, we loaded her again. We had put just eight balls aboard, and powder enough, but no more.

Now they opened a port upon our side and ran out a gun. Kneeling, I took aim with my long-bow and put an arrow through the open port. It must have startled them, although I doubt if damage was done.

We turned right in toward the *Jack*, firing the second time as we lined out straight with a good shot at her. This time our shot was high. It hit the after-house just abaft the wheel.

Almost at the same instant, a *Jack* gun boomed and a shot splashed only a few feet away from us. We were much less of a target than the *Jack*, and before they could put a rammer down her muzzle, we had turned under her stern and come up on the portside, but too close for any gun to reach us.

Men rushed to the rail with small arms. Jublain killed one with a pistol shot. They put their helm hard over to run us down, but Sakim had forseen the move and was already moving away, then falling back.

Somebody ran aft and fired a futile shot at us, and then there was another boom. We saw smoke lifting from the muzzle of one of the stern guns on the *Tiger*. One, then another.

We did not see what effect the *Tiger*'s guns had, but maneuvered close to stay out of range of the *Jack*'s stern guns. Men came aft with muskets.

I put an arrow into the first one, missed the second, and then suddenly, I swore.

Sakim turned and looked at me. "What?" he asked.

"We are fools, Sakim. We forget the obvious."

They were all looking at me now.

"The rudder," I said, "it's point-blank range. Smash their rudder."

Jublain had finished reloading the gun. "All right. Ready when you are."

"Take her in close, Sakim." I held my bow with an arrow notched.

The *Jolly Jack* was swinging now to bring her star-b'rd guns to bear on the *Tiger*.

We ran in as close as we dared. Jublain touched the match to the hole. There was an instant of deadly silence while we waited, then the smash and concussion of the gun.

The four-pound ball hit the rudder post and smashed it. Hastily, Jublain loaded again. It was a pleasure to watch the man, for it was obvious he was a gunner who knew his business, and he worked smoothly, without hesitation or fumble. Again the gun bellowed . . . and the rudder hung loose. The ship looming over us began to fall away.

Sakim was already turning our gig away. For an instant, close in to the vessel, we lost the wind. Then it filled our sails and the gig glided out from the shadow of the ship. A couple of shots barked heavily, balls hit near us, one striking splinters from the gunwhale, but our gig handled smoothly and we sailed away.

Glancing back I saw the *Jolly Jack* had turned broadside to the shore, her guns no longer able to bear on the *Tiger*, some of the crew desperately trimming sail, others working at the stern to rig some kind of a jury rudder.

The *Tiger* had floated free! Now her crew were trying to work her offshore. She had some canvas up, and the longboat was again towing her. As she turned, the *Tiger* let go with two guns, both shots taking effect in the *Jack*'s rigging: a yard came crashing to her deck. And then the *Tiger*'s sails filled and she gathered speed.

The longboat cut loose and dropped back to be picked up.

Further out upon the water we waited, watching the *Jack*. Bardle was a seaman. I'll give him that. He was using his canvas to keep her headed right, and his men were working feverishly. The *Tiger* moved in close to us and a seaman tossed us a line. Sakim

151

made it fast and Corvino rigged the sling on our gun. With another line aft we held our gig close to the *Tiger*'s side, as the gun was hoisted aboard and our own towline made fast.

I was the last man to go aboard, and for a moment I clung to the rope and glanced shoreward. Dark and green was the distant forest, green of trees against the pale sandhills closer by, and blue the water. It was a fair land . . . a fair land. I would leave it with reluctance.

Hand over hand I went up the rope and the gig fell behind on its towrope. Tempany was on the quarterdeck, with Abigail close beside him.

"Neat work, Sackett," he said, "very neat work."

We pointed our bows to the north and east, looking for a way to the open sea. Tempany had traded along the coast before coming to where we had met, and his trade had gone well. I had furs . . . enough to pay me well for my time, yet I wanted more and we had the space for it.

"What now?" Jublain asked me.

"We'll sail north," I said, "but if I prevail we'll go into that big bay * north of here, cut some mast timbers and burn driftwood for potash."

And so we did. On the shores of the large bay we found standing timber, and we cut several for ships' masts, burning wood the meanwhile until we had forty tons of potash to add to our cargo. There had been, meanwhile, more trade with Indians nearby.

Dealing with Indians I found them of shrewd intelligence, quick to detect the false, quick to appreciate quality, quick to resent contempt and to appreciate bravery. So much of the Indian's life was predi-

---

* Chesapeake Bay.

cated upon courage that he respected it above all else. He needed courage in the hunt, and in warfare, and to achieve success within the tribe he needed both courage and wit.

We kept to smaller bays and river-mouths, hoping not to be found by Bardle. But we knew he would be looking. He was better gunned than we, and had a far larger crew, and fighting men all of them.

At last, our holds filled to the bursting with furs, potash and timber, we set sail for England.

"It will be good to be home," Abigail said, at supper.

"Yes," I agreed, reluctantly, "but I shall come back to these shores."

Tempany looked up from his soup. "If we come safely back to England," he said, "you will realize a goodly sum."

"Yes," I agreed.

"And you have friends there, awaiting your return."

"That is possible," I said carefully, "but I place no faith in such things. My future is one I must make myself, this I know. And my future, I think, is back there."

"Gosnold will be sailing again, and there was talk of what Raleigh might do. So many have disappeared in that wilderness . . . We have been very fortunate."

We discussed much during the long and often stormy nights that followed. We talked of a trading post, of a place in London, on the docks, a place from which to sell or ship our goods. With a man in London, Tempany commanding the ships, and myself in America, we could soon build such a business.

"Who for London?" Tempany said, frowning. "I have been so long away that I know few men."

"I know the man," I said quietly. "He is a rogue, but an honest man withal. I speak of Peter Tallis."

"You spoke of him. Is he to be trusted?"

"I believe so. I would trust him if he gave us his word . . . and he is shrewd. He knows business, he knows people, he is aware of all that goes on in London. We should look far for a better man."

"Talk to him then."

So I intended, and such plans were made, and the plans for the discharge of my cargo, and for sharing with Jublain and Corvino. All this was attended to.

We sailed up the Thames, at last, looking at the lights along the shore. It seemed impossible there could be so many.

Suddenly, Jublain grasped my arm. "Barnabas . . . *look!*"

He pointed, and I felt a shock, then a wave of disquiet and fear.

And well I might.

It was the *Jolly Jack*, come home before us, and by the look of her, here for several days.

Nick Bardle was ashore then, and he would surely have seen Rupert Genester.

They would be waiting for me.

Chapter 18

River men came alongside, calling up to take us ashore, but Tempany would have none of them. "They are a hard lot, good men many of them, arrant thieves many others. We will take no risk. We'll take our own boat ashore."

He glanced at me. "Do you take care. I am ashore to speak of my voyage and our success, as well as to lay plans for our next."

"Corvino is off to the Walk for Peter Tallis," I said, "and I shall go to the Tabard and send word to my friend Hasling. If Tallis does not know the state of affairs, Hasling will."

As we descended into our boat some of the river men cursed us for not using theirs, and then vanished toward their berths. One boat lingered, seeming to follow us.

"Aye," Jublain said gloomily, "we be nearing trouble again."

On English soil again, Tempany and Abigail were off to their home, and I and my friend to the Tabard. If Genester wanted me, let him come. The arrogance of success was on me.

We walked into the dark and narrow streets, picking our way over the broken cobbles, and around refuse thrown into the streets from the buildings along the way. A rat scurried from underfoot, and the shadows seemed to move.

Jublain moved nearer. "I like it not, Barnabas. I have the stink of death in my nostrils."

"Not our death," I replied quietly. "If there is death tonight it will be another who dies."

"Let us hope," he commented dryly.

My hand was on my sword hilt, and Jublain carried a naked dagger in his left hand, close down to his side, his right hand on his sword hilt. But nothing happened. We emerged from a dark street into a lighter one, somewhat wider, and Jublain sheathed his dagger with a sigh.

Glancing back suddenly my eye was quick enough to see a shadow fade into an alleyway, yet there were many abroad at such a time who had no wish to be seen, some of them honest men. Yet I knew what Jublain meant by having the smell of death in his nostrils. I had it, as well.

The Tabard was lighted and the inn yard itself had light from its windows.

We squeezed in, and found for ourselves a corner. It was not wine I wanted this night but a tankard of ale, for my throat was dry from walking the shadowed streets.

The ale was brought us, and at further urging and a coin to grease the wheels, several thick slices of ham, a loaf, and several large apples. We were hungry, ravenously so.

There was a square-shouldered, apple-cheeked maid I recalled from before—easily recalled, because she had eyes for Jublain, for all his sallow manner.

She came near to our table. Well enough she remembered me, and Jublain as well. "There is a message," she whispered. "It was left for you but two days past. Sit you, and I will have it down to you."

She had scarcely stopped by the table, almost as if

held up by the press about us, and then she was gone. "A likely lass," I said, grinning at Jublain.

He shrugged his shoulders and stared into his ale. "Aye," he said, "I have a fear of such. Those who would rob you or trick you are easy enough to handle, but such as her . . . A man has small chance with such as her."

"I'd best look for a new partner then," I said, "for certain it is she has set her cap for you."

There was a man with a tankard at a table nearby, a red-faced fellow with a shock of uncombed hair and blond eyebrows. A wide face he had, and thick hands that needed washing. He was looking everywhere but at us but I had an idea he was listening, despite the tumult.

"There's a pitcher near," I commented, as I lifted my tankard, "with big handles."

Jublain's eyes were cynically amused. His back was to the man. "Would a sweep of my sword take him?"

"Aye, but it's a surly rogue we have there, and I think his handles are picking up nothing. I think we should let the pitcher be until we see whether it stands alone."

"I suppose," Jublain said, "but I would like to slice off enough to bait a fish and feed it to him."

Soon the red-cheeked girl came by again, bringing each of us a fresh tankard of ale. She leaned far over.

"Pay for this," she said. "I am watched."

We paid out the money, and she put her hand on the table to pick it up, dropping a folded bit of paper on the table. I casually covered it with my hand. When she had gone, we ate for a bit, and drank. The last thing I wished to do was bring ill to this girl who wished to help.

Then without lifting the paper from the table, I

157

spread open its folds. I knew the hand in which it was written, and read aloud:

There is an order for your arrest. The one of whom we spoke is dying. You will be thrown into prison or killed. We are doing what we can. The one who would help has been taken to the country, and is held there, supposedly to give him the best of care. No one is permitted to see him.

C.H.

"There's a pretty kettle of fish!" I said.

"It be that," said Jublain.

"Come, let's be away from here," I got hurriedly to my feet, and at that instant a hand touched my sleeve.

The red-cheeked maid was there. "This way," she said. "They are in front who would harm you."

We followed quickly, weaving through the tables and the crowd until we reached a dark, narrow passage that led not to the inn-yard but to an empty field beyond. She pointed out a dim path. "Go," she whispered. "There is a path to the river!"

We went, and at a goodly pace. I wanted no lying in prison, for there were those who had stayed shut away for years for no just cause.

The path was sloping away down a small hill, into a hollow and then to the river not far hence. We came down to a place among the reeds, and followed along to a landing place.

It was an old wharf, long disused, it's timbers broken in places to where one could see the gleam of dark water below. No boats were there. Reeds had grown up about the place, and the river flowed by, dark and mysterious.

From far behind us there was the slam of the inn door, then the door opened again and we could see a shaft of light. "It is the only way!" Somebody shouted loudly. "They have gone to the river!"

"Nonsense!" The second voice was more forceful. "There's no escape that way, unless they can swim the Thames."

But he was wrong.

There was a path, and we took it.

Walking up the muddy slope to the embankment, we strolled, arm in arm, talking of the New World and what we had seen there, of London and the meals at the Tabard. We were both dry as sin, and would have relished a bit of ale. We walked along, strolling as along a boulevard, not two men escaping from the Queen's officers.

"Wait, Jublain. I think we are followed."

He glanced around. "Aye, and there are but two of them. Shall we split them, my friend, and give them to Mother Thames? She has taken much refuse at one time or another, and floats fine ships in spite of it."

"Walk on. There are lights ahead, and who is going to question two strolling gentlemen?"

"With muddy boots?"

"That, in some places, might be questioned. Not in London today. There are a deal of places where a gentleman might get his boots muddy. Look, there's a tavern!"

It had a seedy, down-at-the-heels look about it, a rank sort of place, yet the door was welcome. We rounded the building and entered.

A low-beamed ceiling that made me duck my head at the beams, a scattering of benches, a long table, a sort of ledge from which drinks were served and carried to the tables. There were seafaring men there, by the look of them, and some workmen, and a raunchy group in front who looked liked thieves or worse.

They eyed us as we entered, missing nothing. Eyed our boots as well. But we crossed the room and sat down at a table where someone had only just left. Empty tankards stood there. I eased my sword about to an easier place for my hand to fall, and the rascals noticed it.

One of them crossed to our table. He was a slender man with one eye and a patch for the other, a disreputable hat upon his head with a bedraggled plume. His clothing was shabby but he walked with an air and some style.

"Do not rest your hand upon your sword, my friend," he said. "There are thieves present, but we never foul our own nest, and this is our nest, our place. Dainty, is it not? Too much ale is drunk here, and too many bold stories are told by bold chaps who then slink off to some shabby hole to sleep. Only our lives are petty; never our boasts or our dreams."

"There is always hope for a man who can dream, and even for one who can boast, for when the two are together they try to bring both to reality. I speak from experience."

"Say you so? Well, perhaps there is hope then, even hope for me." He glanced at Jublain, and had no doubts about him. He and Jublain were two of a kind, in some ways. Of me he was uncertain. I looked and acted the gentleman, yet I had dirty boots and had come in suddenly out of the night in a disreputable part of town. "You puzzle me . . . so much the gentleman." He said thoughtfully. "Yet your face is weathered from the elements, as no gentleman's is likely to be. I know that look, too, and even in this dim light know a sea-won weathering from that of the heather."

160

He was smiling at me, his eyes mildly amused. "Two who walk on muddy paths in the dark, two only fresh from the sea. And a ship has come up the river, the *Tiger*, only just back from America. And the Queen's men are out to find two from that ship——"

"They will be coming in the door at any moment," I told him frankly.

"Let us exchange hats," he said, "mine is considerably less than yours, but I am of slighter build. Come, let us change."

We did so. His was battered and much worn, and the plume so sad, indeed, but it had a different weight, a different feeling. He donned my own hat, then turned and called out, "Major Sealey! Bring us four, will you? And join us here."

He looked around, smiling. "I am Jeremy Ring, once an officer on Her Majesty's ship, then a prisoner in Barbary and now a homeless, masterless, landless man."

The door opened suddenly and two men stood there. One was a sharp, erect soldierly man, the other a stolid-seeming fellow who looked to need a hayfork in his hands more than a musket.

They looked sharply about—their eyes taking in the group of lusty characters near the door, then at us.

Even as their eyes came to rest on us, Sealey crossed to our table with four brimming tankards in his big hands. The sharper of the two looked from the fresh tankards to the empty ones on the table.

I was sitting low on my bench to appear the shorter, and the hat of Jeremy Ring evidently gave me a different look. It was my own hat upon which his eyes fastened when he looked at Ring. "You there!" he demanded. "How long have you been here?"

"Twenty-seven years, Captain. Born within sound of the Bow-Bells. Twenty-seven years, and seventeen of them aboard Her Majesty's ships or in her army ashore."

"I mean here . . . in this place."

"Oh? A few minutes. We are just over from the Tabard. We found the place crowded, and needed room to bend an elbow. Will you join us, Captain? We will talk of wars and women, the worries of one, the wiles of the other."

"I have no time for that. I am on the Queen's business."

Jeremy looked shocked. "The Queen has business *here*? In such a place? My dear fellow, I am surprised, I——"

"No, no, you fool! I am looking for two Her Majesty would arrest."

"Only two? I could name a dozen, Captain, even a dozen dozen who richly deserve arrest. Why, I could name a Queen's officer, Captain, who deserves to be quartered, drawn and quartered, at the very least.

"Come, Captain. Sit down, buy us a round of drinks and I will tell you such a tale——"

"You are a fool! I've no time for that." He stared angrily at Ring. "You just came from the Tabard? Then we waste time, Robert. Obviously we have followed the wrong men."

"It was dark, and the hat——"

"To the devil with the hat! There are many such!" They turned angrily, shoved their way through the door and were gone.

Jeremy Ring turned to me, smiling. "Now? You will pay for the ale, will you not?"

"I will," I said, "and gladly."

"We will finish the ale," he said, "and then I shall take you to a house nearby——"

"We wish only shelter, a place to sleep."

"What else? The lady is a sailor's wife, and you know how it is with them when her Jack is long gone and there's the need to live. The best places, the cleanest places in London are kept by sailor's wives, often enough."

"So I have heard."

"Mag is a good girl, one of the best, and she had a big old house willed to her by an uncle, or father, or grandfather . . . anyway, she lets rooms.

"She talks a bit, but not about her guests. Come, finish your ale, those two might come back, or others."

There was a light in a window of the tall house on the corner. "That'll be Mag. She reads, poor girl. Sits up with reading or sewing, and there's too many do the last and too few the first."

Mag was a comely lass with blue eyes and a steady way about her, as she held high the lantern and regarded us coolly. "If you be friends of Jeremy you are welcome." She looked severely from Jublain to me. "But being friends of Jeremy you'll pay in advance. And now, before you've come a step further. He owes me enough himself without bringing others to sleep under my roof and eat my fare without a penny toward the cost."

"How much?"

"A six-pence, if you sleep in one bed, six-pence for each if you will have two. There's some as sleep four and five to the bed, so for them its a tuppence each."

"Two beds," I said, "and we'll be wanting a taste of something in the morning."

I placed a shilling in her hand. "Take that," I said,

163

"and another for good measure, and worry none at all about us."

"I'll not worry," she said pertly, "and if you are thinking it's a woman alone, I am, do not think twice about it, for I am never alone." From under her robe, tied by a string, she lifted a heavy pistol. "And if you think he will not speak for me, come to my door when the lights are out. You will have a bellyful of him."

"I do not doubt it," I said, smiling at her, "and if you had not a husband away on a ship, I'd be tempted to talk you into throwing your pistol out the window."

She looked at me boldly. "That would take more talking than you've the tongue for, but come. I'll show you to your beds."

The rooms were small, but surprisingly clean and pleasant. As she turned away I stopped her. "Jeremy Ring? You have known him long?"

"He is a good man," she said flatly, "a bold man, and a witty one, but a good man. A good master on a ship, too, it is said, but times be bad and he was too long a prisoner in Barbary. There's few who know him now."

"I shall be having need of him, I think." From my pocket I took a guinea. "I do not know how much he owes, but put that against it——"

"It is too much."

"Then he will have food to eat and a bed to sleep in for a bit longer."

"You are a good man," she said quietly, "a good man. I bless you for him."

My boots were off and I was soon undressed, and weary to the death. I stretched out upon the bed and drew high the covers. A sleep I would have this night, if never again.

My eyes closed, and then they opened again and looked into the dark. I must venture to look in upon my father's old friend. How could I leave him sick and helpless in the hands of Rupert Genester?

Chapter 19

We Sacketts were always good men at table, and I no less than the others. So when time came, I put foot under the table of the sailor's wife and set to with a loaf of dark, rich bread and some rashers of bacon and slices of cheese.

Jeremy Ring and Jublain were with me, both doing justice to what was placed before us.

"I must know where he is," I said. "I must do something for him."

"You do not even know the man," Jublain grumbled. "You'll stick your nose into a trap for a man to whom you've never spoken."

"My father and he fought side by side. My father would have died for him. Can I do less?"

"They were in a fight together. It is a different thing. If you go into a fight with a man, you stay by him until he is dead or a prisoner."

"Aye, but who will stand by a sick old man whose death is desired? I shall go to him, Jublain, but I shall ask no man to walk beside me. The place to which I shall go is one I can enter alone."

"It is a trap, and you are a fool."

"We have a failing the fen-men do. Others may not

165

like us, some say we smell of our fens, some say we are a dark mysterious, murderous lot, but we have a failing that is our own. We are loyal. We stand by each other . . . or have until now."

"You talk in words that are vain," Jublain said irritably. "You do not know where he is."

"But we shall find out, shall we not? Jeremy, you could do this for me. I sent my man Corvino to Peter Tallis. By this time he may know where the old man is, but Coveney Hasling would know, if anyone does."

Ring got up immediately. "Good enough! I shall pass the word to a carter I know who is returning up-country, and he shall carry the word to Hasling."

Jublain looked sour. "We should catch a boat and be down the river by dusk. There are ships off the Downs that will need men. And you've money."

"I've little. Our goods are not sold and until then it's little enough I have."

For two days we waited in Mag's house. Then suddenly one day a boat drifted up to a landing near the house and two men came up from it to the door. One was Corvino, the other was Hasling.

"Where is he?" I asked.

Hasling shrugged, and dropped upon a bench. "You are in trouble enough, and the old man is far gone. Too far, I fear, for him to do aught about a will now."

"Bother the will! I want the man safe and comfortable his last days. I shall make enough myself not to need what he would offer me, and it is so I would have it."

Hasling leaned across the table. "Genester came to him the instant he was ill, and made much of his illness and the proper care that was due him. 'I will take him to the seashore,' was what he said, 'and the good sea air will bring him his strength again!' And so he took him away, and in London all are saying what a fine nephew Genester is, to think so of his old uncle . . ."

"Where has he taken him?" I asked.

Hasling shrugged. "Where, indeed? He has told no one. And when they ask, Genester says the Earl is poorly, but will improve with rest and care . . . No visitors, no disturbances, just rest."

" 'No visitors?' "

Corvino snapped his fingers. "Hah! Give me a day, two days even, and I will know where they have gone. There are no secrets from me in London!

"If he traveled, being ill, it was by carriage or by wagon. And how many carriages have there been in London in the last few years? And how many of those would he have access to? And which of those were not otherwise in use at that time? Give me the time, and——"

"You have the time," I told him, "what I want is the where . . . and quickly."

When he was gone, Hasling looked at me curiously. "You make friends, Barnabas. It is a fine thing to make so many friends."

"They are good men." I leaned forward. "You should have been with us to see the New World. It is beautiful! There are fields, forests, mountains, streams!"

"You did well?"

"I did, and shall go back, too. It's a fair land, Coveney Hasling, and perhaps it is there I will stay."

"But the savages?"

I shrugged. "I will be friendly with those who are friendly, and I will fight those who wish to fight. I would trade with the Indians, but I see the danger in it. Yet when two peoples come together that one which is most efficient will survive, and the other will absorb or vanish . . . it is the way of life.

"The Indian must not lose pride in what he does, in his handicraft, for if he loses pride he will no longer build, his art will fail him, and he will completely be dependent upon others."

Hasling nodded. "It is well to think of these things, yet I believe few will listen . . . or care. The problem now, when you discover where our friend is, is what you can do."

"I shall fetch him and take him where he can have proper care."

"You must beware. Rupert Genester has friends at court, nor is he a fool. Suppose you fetched the Earl away from him and he dies on your hands?"

It was a thought that had not come to me.

"Do you see what I mean? Genester would then have attained both his desires. The old man would be dead, and you would go to prison, a kidnapper."

"Nevertheless, he was my father's friend. It is a weakness of my family that we do not forget our friends. I cannot let him die so. He must be among friends."

"Look," Hasling said patiently, "please understand. Since you have been gone, the situation has changed. Not only is your friend ill, but Rupert Genester has advanced himself. He is skilled at flattery, he knows for whom favors are to be done, and he has worked himself into a secure position at court. He belongs to no group, no clique, no party, yet has done favors for all, so each one can hope that, when Genester inherits, he will be *their* friend, *their* partisan."

Hasling paused. "He has closed all doors for you. Not intentionally—for he did not believe you would return, until the *Jolly Jack* came with news of your escape.

"Nor can Brian Tempany help you. He is in deep trouble because of talk that Genester circulated. The Queen ordered your arrest. Tempany himself may be arrested at any moment, and be assured, my friend, if you go to prison you will not emerge."

"There is a ship for the Low Country in the morning," Jublain said, "and I know its captain. We can be aboard before daybreak, and down the river before it is realized we are gone."

"It is a good thought," Hasling said. "The temper of the Queen will change. She is an uncommonly shrewd woman, and will not long be fooled by Genester."

Yet I was worried. I had heard many a tale of what men of influence had been able to bring about in getting rid of enemies, and the Queen only knew what was told her. A good woman, a fine woman, and an excellent Queen, yet she could not be everywhere at once, could not investigate each story she was told. She relied upon advisors, and they had their own loyalties.

Rupert Genester had such friends as I would never have, and others who were loyal to him because of his birth and background. He was an aristocrat, a man apart.

"All right," I said at last, "the Low Countries, but we shall make one stop first."

At that moment, Corvino entered. With him was Peter Tallis.

"It is good to see you," said Tallis. "And the charts? Were they of value?"

"Very much so. What I wish to know is where the Earl has been taken. Someone has said that it was to the seashore."

"Then my information may be correct," Tallis said. He paused. "Do you know a deep valley to the South of London?"

"No," I said. "I think not. . . ."

"I know the area well," said Ring. "When I was a younger man I often visited there."

"There's an old manor, a fortified place. It's a couple of hundred years old—belonged to a rich, doughty old warrior, but a part of it is in ruins now. I hear Genester has taken the Earl there."

"That could be," Ring said thoughtfully, "I know the old place . . . fourteenth century or earlier. Rupert Genester had relatives who once lived along the coast there, and I know the George Inn."

"I, too," said Jublain. "I have been there."

"My story is they have taken him there," Tallis said, "along with two servants in Genester's hire, and several guards to 'protect' the Earl."

"Is it near the coast?" I asked.

"A few miles, but there is a river that can be navigated . . . at least that far. Below the Forelands. In fact, that may have been why the old place was built, to stop invasion along the river in olden times," Tallis said.

"We'll do it then. Jublain, you know the gig and the manor. Down the river within the hour, around the Forelands and up the river. Corvino will go with you."

"He was my friend, too," Hasling said. "I must be one of you."

"No," I said. "Does the Earl have a trustworthy friend here? One who has no use for Genester?"

"He does. I can take him to a most powerful man who will guard him well."

"Then see this man, make the arrangements, and we will come, if God wills."

"And you?" Hasling asked.

"I shall ride across country, with Ring to show the way." I glanced over at Tallis. "I will need horses. Can it be arranged?"

"It can. I shall be with you."

"No. Do you stay and dispose of my goods. We shall need money and a ship to the New World, for when this is over I fear there will be no place in England for me for some time to come.

"However," I added, "there will be consignments of furs. Brian Tempany and I have talked of you, Peter. Are you with us?"

"We met, we talked, we agreed. I am with you indeed."

A few more details and all was ready. I went to my room and buckled on sword and pistols, gathering the well-filled saddlebags.

Mag came to the door. "There's some'at to eat there," she said. "You'll be needing it."

"If they find this place, Mag," I said, "you know nothing of me or any of us. We came here and stopped the night and then were gone. I kept to myself and acted worried. You were glad when I was gone."

"If I were a man, I'd ride with you."

I smiled at her. "Mag, if you were a man, we'd all regret it. Do you be the woman you are, and wait for that sailorman who'll be coming back soon."

I put a gold coin in her hand. "If any of the others come back and need help, give it to them."

Only a short distance for Ring and myself to where the horses waited, then into the saddle, and a sound of hoofs on cobbles, and then we were off, guided down dark lanes by Jeremy Ring.

171

Two men with swords, daggers, and pistols, two men riding on a fool's mission, to the aid of a man neither one of us knew. He had stood in battle beside my father, my father had spent blood with him upon more than one field, but I had not seen him. And Jeremy Ring?

He rode because he was Jeremy Ring, a gallant follower of lost or flimsy causes, a poet with a sword, a man for whom life was a thing to be nobly used, not allowed to rust or wither and decay. He had missed his chances elsewhere, this one he would not miss.

At a pause atop a hill, our horses had time to breathe and catch their wind.

"Jeremy," I said, "if we come through this, there's the New World yonder. Will you be sailing with me?"

"Aye . . . Wherever you go."

We rode on then, following a dim track into the night, and I thought of Abigail, waiting, and of our first meeting on the dark night after my flight from the theater.

I thought of her and our few talks aboard ship, of things longed for and sought, of things dreamed of and wanted.

Through a dark wood with a smell of damp earth and damper leaves, to the drum of hoofs upon the turf, and the low murmur of wind in the branches above.

Would the old man, the Earl, be dead? Did Genester actually intend to simply let him die? Or to hasten his death?

Chapter 20

Jeremy Ring was a better horseman than I, for I had walked more than I had ridden. Moreover, he knew the roads.

Before we had gone a dozen miles I was totally lost, Jeremy did so much weaving about. We had no wish to be followed, so he made sudden diversions down lanes between cottages or around barns and even through pastures, and several times we paused to listen.

"You know the way well," I said, with a tinge of suspicion.

He chuckled. "I should, my friend, for I've worked the King's highways upon more than one occasion. I would say that to you and no other, but the truth is in me tonight."

The night was damp and cool. After resting the horses a bit we rode on, taking more time now that we were well away from London.

We came to a slope and, crossing a small valley, we started up a winding ridge toward a village above. "There's a man here and a tavern," Ring said, "a friendly man if you have a coin or two, who will switch horses and forget it."

SEVENOAKS, a sign said. There were trees, but I could see no oaks.

We had slices of cold ham and the end of a loaf

and slept the night out. In the morning, on a pair of matching bays, we rode along the ridge to the eastward, skirting the knoll, then circling about, as Jeremy was of no mind to let them know our direction.

The sun was out and the day was warm, our destination still some distance.

We saw no one, nor wished to.

We stopped at last near an abandoned woodcutter's hut, deep in the woods. There was a well nearby, and the ruins of some much older building. We tied our horses and waited for the dark. Through the thinnest of the foliage we could see the squarecut outlines of the manor, not more than a half mile off.

At dusk we mounted and walked our horses through the woods, keeping off the paths until we reached the bank of the river. The willows were thick along the banks. Dismounting, we led our horses down and let them drink.

Suddenly, we heard the faintest of sounds. Someone was coming along the bank just outside the clumps of willows, a bit higher up. It was someone who moved cautiously.

He appeared then, not far off, yet easily seen in the dim light. He paused, and I spoke.

"Ah?" It was Jublain. "I was sure you would be here." He came toward us through the trees. "The boat is tied to the bank not a cable-length from here. Should we be closer?"

"Yes. Corvino is on the boat?"

"Corvino and Sakim. Without Sakim we would not have made it so soon. He is a fine sailor, that one."

"Aye. Then leave him with the boat and do you and Corvino come with me."

"There is a landing below the house. Should we come there?"

"Aye, and soon. What is to be done must be done quickly, smoothly." For a moment I listened into the silence. "I will meet you at the landing. Come quickly."

He turned swiftly away and, with Jeremy following, I led my horse back through the woods. Soon the manor loomed above us, and we could see the gleam of water on our right and the gray of a path that led down to the landing. Good enough.

We tied our horses well back into the trees, and waited for Jublain and Corvino. I had no worries about Sakim. He was perhaps the wisest of us all, and would not be taken unawares. We went up the path in single file.

The night had grown increasingly dark. Stars gleamed above although there were a few drifting clouds. It was damp and still. Picking our way over the fallen stones and the remnants of a wall we found a door. It was closed and locked. When I felt of the lock my fingers came away with cobwebs. An unused door, evidently barred from within.

Moss covered the fallen stones, vines hung from the walls. We rounded the house by a faint path.

Jeremy put a hand on my arm. "I like none of it," he whispered. "The place smells of a trap."

"Aye, but we came to help the Earl. Trap or no trap, we shall do it.'

"There are the stables," Corvino whispered. "Do you wait now." He was gone in an instant, back as soon. "There is a carriage outside, and a dozen horses within. Several of them are still wet with sweat. They have been hard-ridden within the hour."

"A dozen? Perhaps four for the carriage, and eight

175

for outriders or others. They are eight or nine. Perhaps ten."

"It is a goodly number," Ring suggested thoughtfully.

"Enough to go around. Come now, no jealousy! Each of you will have at least one, and two if you are lucky. Gentlemen, I think we are expected. Let us not keep them waiting. As my name is Barnabas Sackett, I hope that Rupert Genester is himself here."

We started forward, then I stopped. "Jeremy? Do you and Corvino mind? Jublain and I will enter alone. Do you follow us. In that way we may not all be trapped at once."

We went forward, up the few steps, and Jublain put a hand to the door. At my gesture, he opened it and I stepped inside. There had been no chain on the door, no bar. Truly, we were expected. Stepping inside, Jublain followed.

The great entranceway was dark and shadowed. Light showed beneath a door. I stepped quickly forward and in that instant the big door slammed behind us and torches flared into light.

We were in the center of a great hall and a dozen men stood about us, all with drawn swords.

One stepped slightly forward. "You do not disappoint me, Sackett. You come quickly to meet your death."

"Of course. Did you expect me to keep you waiting?"

"They've barred the door," Jublain said quietly.

"Aye, that makes it better. Not one of them shall escape us. And look, Jublain. The rascal with the beard. It is Nick Bardle himself, trying to patch up the mistakes he made."

A move, and my blade was drawn. "I hope the Earl is still alive? Or have you murdered him?"

Genester shrugged. "He will die . . . Why hasten it? I want no marks upon *his* body, but on yours——?"

"Of course. Will you try to put them there yourself? Or will you sprawl in the mud again as you did in Stamford?"

His lips tightened with anger, and he took a half-step forward. I held my blade low, smiling at him. "You were a fit sight for a lady, sprawled in all your pretty silks in the mud! There was no occasion for it. The lady but asked for a drink."

"I shall kill you now," he said.

"Will you try it alone? Or leave it to this pack of dogs that follows you?"

Above me, faintly, I heard a scrape of something. A foot on stone? What was above? I dared not look up.

"Do not let him die too quickly," Genester said. "But die he must."

"And you, Rupert? Are you ready for the blade? I've chosen a resting place for it, right under that pretty little beard."

"Take him," he said, and turned indifferently away.

They moved, but I moved first. I was within a long blade's reach of the nearest man and, taking a quick step, I lunged just as his sword came up. There was a faint clang of steel, and my blade went past his and a hand's length into his chest.

His eyes stared at me down the length of the blade, the eyes of a man who would die. I withdrew swiftly and then Jublain shouted, "At them!" And then there was only the clang of swords, the whisper of clothing and the grunt and pant of men fighting.

From above there was a shrill yell, then down a rope came Corvino, and then Jeremy.

A man rushed at me, swinging a cutlass, a wide sweep with a blade that might have been effective in a boarding operation. But not here. My blade was down and I cut swiftly upward. The blade slit through his shirt front and parted his chin—the very stroke I had planned for Genester himself.

At least two were down. I felt a blade nick my arm, the rip of my shirt. It was close, deadly fighting, with no time for fancy work here. I thrust, slashed, thrust again, moving always.

Corvino was down . . . no, up again. There was blood on his shirt. The torchlight wavered and shadowed and unshadowed us. Faces gleamed with sweat. It was wild, desperate, bitter fighting this.

A tall man lunged at me. I parried and he came in with his thrust and we were face to face, our swords locked tightly. It was Darkling.

My left fist came up quickly in a smashing blow to his belly and he gasped and stepped back. I followed him in, keeping our swords locked, and hit him again . . . my attack totally unexpected.

Darkling fell back again, disengaged and tried to come into position. But my own blade was far forward and, without drawing it back, I turned quickly left and cut across his face under his nose, then right, and under his eyes. Neither was deep, both were bloody. He fell back, shocked, and I let him go.

A blade ripped my shirt again and then we were forced into a corner, Jublain and I. Corvino was down or gone. Jeremy was waging a desperate fight with three men, his blade dancing, gleaming, thrusting. One man fell back with a cry, and Jeremy dropped quickly to one knee—or almost there—with a sweeping blow at the next man's legs. Killing him as well.

Suddenly there was a banging upon the door, a shout, and Jeremy skipped quickly to one side and, fencing adroitly to hold the man off, managed to flip the bar from the door. Instantly it crashed open.

Captain Tempany! And with him four men!

Suddenly there was a break for the door, and desperate fighting there. Leaping across a body I raced up the steps to the door through which Genester had gone.

I shoved the door slowly inward and a pistol coughed hoarsely in the small confines of the room. Leaping through the door, sword in hand, I saw Rupert Genester just beyond.

The Earl—at least I supposed him to be—sat up in bed, a woman standing near him, her face pale and angry. Genester threw the now empty pistol at my head and then ran around the end of the bed to come at me.

He was facing me, a desperate man. His face was pale, his eyes very bright and hard. There was no coward in the man, for all I disliked him. His blade was up and he was ready.

Though I had out-maneuvered him often, Genester faced me squarely. "Even if you live to tell it," he said, "they'll not believe you. I will declare that you killed the Earl."

"But he is not dead!" I said. "I——"

His sword was down by his side in his right hand. Suddenly his left held a dagger, and he lifted it to stab down at the old man who lay beside him. His left fist gripping the dagger swung up and back.

I lunged.

The point of my blade took him at mid-chest and thrust toward his left side.

His arm was caught in movement, and my blade sank deep. He turned his head and looked at me, his eyes wide, lips bloodless. "Damn you!" he gasped. "I should have——"

I lowered my point and he slid off it to the floor, blood all about him, his fingers loosening on the dagger. The dagger clattered to the floor.

"Your pardon, Excellency," I said, "forgive this intrusion, but . . . my name is Barnabas Sackett."

"I know who you are," the old man's voice rumbled like a faroff thunder in the small room. "And you are your father's son.

"By the Lord," he said, sitting a little straighter, "as neat a bit of action as ever I saw!"

Suddenly, I realized that Nick Bardle was gone . . . I'd forgotten him.

Gone! I started after him but the old man lifted a hand. "Let him go," he said, "and open the door before they burst it."

The door opened again. Jublain was the first through, sword in hand, then Jeremy Ring and Sakim. Following was Captain Tempany.

Tempany went to him quickly. "How are you, Sir Robert? You're unhurt?"

"I am not hurt," Sir Robert said flatly, "but I've been damnably ill, and if it had not been for Gerta here, who would not be left behind, I'd be dead. Dead and gone. Now get me out of here."

"We've only horses," Tempany protested.

"I've a boat," I said. "Sakim? Can we make Sir Robert comfortable?"

"Of course."

180

Sir Robert glared at him. "Moor, aren't you? Well, I've crossed swords with a few of your kind."

Sakim smiled, showing his white, even teeth. "I am glad it was not with me, Sir Robert."

The Earl glared, then chuckled. "So am I, so am I. Make a litter, Tempany, and get me out of here. I despise the place."

Chapter 21

Sir Robert sat propped with pillows in the great bed in his town house. Scarce two weeks had passed since the affair in the manor, but the time for decision had come.

Captain Brian Tempany was there, with Abigail. She sat demurely, her hands in her lap.

"I have talked to him, talked like a Dutch uncle, but he will not listen."

Sir Robert eyed me coldly. "His father was a pig-headed man, too." He said, and then added, "Thank God for it. He never knew when he was whipped . . . So he never was."

"It is not that I do not appreciate the offer," I assured him, "but I was born to action. It is not my way to sit contemplating the deeds of others, nor to fatten on wealth not gained by my own hands. There's a vast land yonder, and my destiny lies there. My own destiny, and that of my family."

"This family you speak of," Sir Robert asked gruffly,

"is something of which I have not heard. You are a wedded man?"

"I am not."

"Then you have no family?"

"I do not. I have only the knowledge that some-day I will and that I want them in a land where they may have elbow room. I want my sons to grow tall in freedom, to grow where they may stretch and move and go as far and do as much as their talents and strength will permit. I do not want them ham-strung by privilege nor class."

"You disapprove of England?"

"I do not. Opportunity here is great if a man has energy, but there are restrictions, and I chafe under restriction."

"You must go to America?"

"I must. It is a vast land, every inch of it rich with opportunity. I would go there and build my own place, my own life."

"I will speak to Sir Walter."

"No, Sir Robert. I do not wish that restriction, either. I will go alone . . . Or with those few who would go with me."

Sir Robert glared at me, then glanced at Abigail. "This family you speak of? Where will you find a woman who will leave England for such a wild place? No fine clothes? No dancing, no fine homes? No luxuries? Are there any such?"

"I have reason to believe there are," I said hesi-tantly. "But first I wish to prepare a place . . . a home. I can do it there."

Abigail looked up. "And in the meantime, Bar-nabas?"

I flushed. "Well, I——"

She looked at me coolly, directly—the look she had

given me that first night when she invited me in. "If you know such a girl, I would suggest that you permit her to choose where her home will be. If you find such a girl at all, I imagine she would prefer to be at your side."

"There are savages."

"I presume."

"There are no houses, only caves, and bark shelters."

"I expect that is so."

"I could not ask any——"

"You assume such a girl would have less courage than you? Less fortitude? You do not understand my sex, Barnabas."

"She would be much alone."

"Not for long, I believe. She would have a family if you are half the man you seem to be. I suggest, Barnabas, that when you make your plans for the New World you speak to the lady. You will be gone for a year, and that is a very long time."

"Well, I——"

She turned toward Sir Robert and curtsied. "If you will forgive me, Sir Robert. I must go now and leave the planning to you men. You seem to feel you are perfectly competent to plan for others as well as yourselves."

When the door closed, Sir Robert chuckled. "That young lady knows her mind."

"Her mother was just that way," Brian Tempany said.

"I always said," I commented, "that I wanted a woman to walk beside me, not behind me."

"Have you said that to Abigail?" Tempany asked slyly.

"I haven't, but——"

Sir Robert abruptly changed the subject. "You are determined then? You will sail for America?"

"Aye, when I find a ship." I paused. "Sir Robert, against the western sky there were mountains, blue and distant mountains. I must pass through them. I must see what lies beyond."

"Damme, Sackett, if I was a lad I'd go with you! I'd like myself to see what lies beyond those mountains." He paused. "All right, I'll provide the ship." He looked at me from under fierce brows. "She has a fine cabin aft, a Dutch craft, seaworthy and strong. But a fine cabin, fit for a king—or a queen."

"I will see what I can do."

"Then be about it, lad, and leave the rest to us." He shifted his position a bit. "I've talked to your man Tallis. A good man, Barnabas. He's disposed of your cargo, and has bought well, by your orders."

"Thank you." I was fidgeting, wishing to go. If he saw it he showed it not. "Then, Sir Robert, I shall leave this in your hands, and those of Captain Tempany. I have things——"

"Be off with you!"

She waited in the garden where there were white roses, and red. She waited by a small fountain, and I went to her across the grass. She turned to face me, very serious.

"I was too bold," she said.

"No," I said, "just bold enough to give me courage for boldness. I was afraid I assumed too much."

"You will be gone a year, and that is a very long time. I have seen other girls and women whose men have gone away to sea or to the wars, and they did not come back again. I would not have that happen to me."

"You truly wish to come?"

"Where you are, I would be."

"Sir Robert said the cabin on the boat is a fine one, fit for a queen."

"Hmm! Men know little of what is fit or not fit! I must go aboard at once."

"I will arrange it." I took her hands in mine and kissed her very gently. "And now there is much to do. I must go."

Outside I awaited my carriage. The day had clouded over. And as the carriage came forward, the wheels made grating sounds on the cobbles and a few drops of rain fell.

I was for America again. Soon my own ship would be sailing across the western ocean, back to the land of vast green forests and mountains blue with distance and promise.

I settled back in the cushions, content. The feeling was upon me that in those mountains lay my destiny, whatever it was, however it came.

And Abigail would be with me.

ABOUT THE AUTHOR

LOUIS L'AMOUR, born Louis Dearborn L'Amour, is of French-Irish descent. Although Mr. L'Amour claims his writing began as a "spur-of-the-moment thing," prompted by friends who relished his verbal tales of the West, he comes by his talent honestly. A frontiersman by heritage (his grandfather was scalped by the Sioux), and a universal man by experience, Louis L'Amour lives the life of his fictional heroes. Since leaving his native Jamestown, North Dakota, at the age of fifteen, he's been a longshoreman, lumberjack, elephant handler, hay shocker, flume builder, fruit picker, and an officer on tank destroyers during World War II. And he's written four hundred short stories and over fifty books (including a volume of poetry).

Mr. L'Amour has lectured widely, traveled the West thoroughly, studied archaeology, compiled biographies of over one thousand Western gunfighters, and read prodigiously (his library holds more than two thousand volumes). And he's watched thirty-one of his westerns as movies. He's circled the world on a freighter, mined in the West, sailed a dhow on the Red Sea, been shipwrecked in the West Indies, stranded in the Mojave Desert. He's won fifty-one of fifty-nine fights as a professional boxer and pinch-hit for Dorothy Kilgallen when she was on vacation from her column. Since 1816, thirty-three members of his family have been writers. And, he says, "I could sit in the middle of Sunset Boulevard and write with my typewriter on my knees; temperamental I am not."

Mr. L'Amour is re-creating an 1865 Western town, christened Shalako, where the borders of Utah, Arizona, New Mexico, and Colorado meet. Historically authentic from whistle to well, it will be a live, operating town, as well as a movie location and tourist attraction.

Mr. L'Amour now lives in Los Angeles with his wife Kathy, who helps with the enormous amount of research he does for his books. Soon, Mr. L'Amour hopes, the children (Beau and Angelique) will be helping too.